FIRE STORM

FIRE STORM

BOOK 3

THE ELEMENTAL SERIES

SHANNON MAYER

USA TODAY BESTSELLING AUTHOR OF RECURVE

Firestorm (The Elemental Series, Book 3)
Copyright © Shannon Mayer 2015
Copyright © HiJinks Ink Publishing, Ltd. 2015

All rights reserved Published by HiJinks Ink LTD.
www.shannonmayer.com

All rights reserved. Without limiting the rights under copyright reserved above, no part of this publication may be reproduced, stored in or introduced into a database and retrieval system or transmitted in any form or any means (electronic, mechanical, photocopying or otherwise)without the prior written permission of both the owner of the copyright and the above publishers. Please do not participate in or encourage the piracy of copyrighted materials in violation of the author's rights. Purchase only authorized editions.

This is a work of fiction. Names, characters, places and incidents are either the product of the author's imagination or are used fictitiously, and any resemblance to actual persons living or dead, business establishments, events or locales is entirely coincidental. Or deliberately on purpose, depending on whether or not you have been nice to the author.

Original illustrations by Damonza.com
Mayer, Shannon

Acknowledgments

To all those who have dived without hesitation into Lark's world. Thank you for believing in me as a writer, and in Lark as your new heroine. Firestorm couldn't have come about without Tina Winograd, Jean Faganello (aka Mom), Lysa Lessieur and Damonza (cover art). Thank you for helping me bring yet another story into the light. Or in this case, into the flames . . .

ALSO BY SHANNON MAYER

THE RYLEE ADAMSON NOVELS

Priceless (A Rylee Adamson Novel, Book 1)
Immune (A Rylee Adamson Novel, Book 2)
Raising Innocence (A Rylee Adamson Novel Book 3)
Shadowed Threads (A Rylee Adamson Novel, Book 4)
Blind Salvage (A Rylee Adamson Novel, Book 5)
Tracker (A Rylee Adamson Novel, Book 6)
Veiled Threat (A Rylee Adamson Novel, Book 7)
Wounded (A Rylee Adamson Novel, Book 8)
Rising Darkness (A Rylee Adamson Novel, Book 9)
Blood of the Lost (A Rylee Adamson Novel, Book 10)
Alex (A Rylee Adamson Short Story)
Tracking Magic (A Rylee Adamson Novella 0.25)
Elementally Priceless (A Rylee Adamson Novella 0.5)
Guardian (A Rylee Adamson Novella 6.5)
Stitched (A Rylee Adamson Novella 8.5)

THE ELEMENTAL SERIES

Recurve (The Elemental Series, Book 1)
Breakwater (The Elemental Series, Book 2)
Firestorm (The Elemental Series, Book 3)

THE BLOOD BORNE SERIES
(Written With Denise Grover Swank)

Recombinant (The Blood Borne Series, Book 1)

PARANORMAL ROMANTIC SUSPENSE

The Nevermore Trilogy
Sundered (The Nevermore Trilogy, Book 1)
Bound (The Nevermore Trilogy, Book 2)
Dauntless (The Nevermore Trilogy, Book 3)

URBAN FANTASY

A Celtic Legacy Trilogy
Dark Waters (A Celtic Legacy, Book 1)
Dark Isle (A Celtic Legacy, Book 2)
Dark Fae (A Celtic Legacy, Book 3)

CONTEMPORARY ROMANCES
(Written as S.J. Mayer)

High Risk Love (The Risk Series, Book 1)
Of The Heart

Chapter 1

agma's hands dug into my arms, pinning them back at an angle sharp enough that my shoulders threatened to pop out of joint. Around us, the redwoods of the Rim swayed, the trunks groaning as the wind pushed at them. In the distance a long howl of a wolf made me think for just a moment that maybe Griffin would come back and help Ash and me escape the hold the Salamanders—aka fire elementals—had on us. But there was no sound of running pads on the ground, no snarl of a wolf as he attacked our captors to help free us.

I shouldn't have been surprised. A month past, Ash and I had gone into the fire elementals' home, the Pit, in search of a cure for the lung burrowers that were wiping out our people. We'd been turned away, but I didn't take no for an answer. Ultimately, we did find the cure, and our family was saved. But the cost was high and there were several deaths. All at the end of my spear. For a time, I'd thought we'd escaped punishment.

I scanned the forest looking for any sign of movement and saw none; there was no one coming to our rescue, no one coming to tell the Salamanders to let us go. Though we were in the Rim, we were once again on our own. Apparently even my father had given up on me, handing us over to Queen Fiametta and the Pit after specifically telling me he would never do that to any of his children. How quickly things changed in my life and my understanding of those around me.

Again.

Turning my head slowly, making myself not react to the pain, I glared at Maggie.

"Maggie, we've already said we'd go with you."

She snorted, her orange eyes narrowing. "Magma, not Maggie, we are *not* friends." Her fingernails cut into my bare skin, and trickles of warm blood slid down my upper arms into the crooks of my elbows. "A liar like you can't be trusted, so I think we'll be doing things my way." The other three Enders with her laughed, but I didn't even look at them. They were not my problem at the moment. She tightened her hold on me as if to emphasize the point that she was indeed in charge.

I made myself smile through the throbbing ache in my upper back and shoulders and took a shot in the dark. "Your fellow Enders don't think much of you, do they? Letting me slip into the Pit, then escape while you just stood there and watched must have really set you down in the ranks. Especially since I'm just a lowly earth elemental."

From the right of me, Ash let out a low groan. "Lark, don't push her."

But it was too late for taking the words back, and I

wouldn't have anyway, not after everything Ash and I had been through in the Deep. After surviving the world of the Undines—water elementals—I wasn't sure I had it in me to be patient or forgiving of anyone who didn't have Terraling—earth elemental—blood running through their veins.

Maggie, Magma to me now if I let her have her way, let out a low rumbling hiss, the sound reminiscent of a bellows in a forge. "When they execute you, the smile on my face will be the last thing you see."

I looked away from her, but the scene around me didn't give much hope. The Enders surrounding us were dressed in black from head to toe, their ensembles completed by their long black cloaks, and three-foot-long narrow black clubs that hung from their belts. Unlike our Ender clothes that consisted of dark and light browns, a vest and pants, the Enders from the pit were covered up entirely. Right down to the thick black boots they wore. If it weren't for their varying shades of brilliant red hair, they would have been monotone from top to bottom.

The Ender holding Ash glared at me and I realized I knew him too. We'd met before. "Match?"

He'd been with Maggie when they'd met us at the door of the Pit when all we'd wanted was help from their healers. He'd fought us, as had Maggie, and that started what ultimately led me to kill not one or two, but *four* of the Pit's Enders.

"Don't talk to me," he growled, baring his teeth at me. "You aren't getting away from us this time. Your sentencing is going to be swift, and even your king can't deny us this right." I realized, as he glared at me, that Maggie wasn't the only one who'd been made to look like a fool.

Maggie's words, and his finally, sank into my mind. The sentence for one Ender killing another was very simple.

Death at the hands of the offended party, which in my case was the Pit. Magma dragged me forward a few steps alongside Ash. He caught my eye. "Just follow my lead."

Match cuffed him in the head, hard enough to split the skin over his left eye. "Shut your filthy mouth, Terraling."

Ash's mouth twitched and he glared at Match. "Brave boy now that you have all your friends with you."

Match grunted as if he'd been punched. "I warned you."

The Ender slid his long black club from his belt and swung it toward Ash. As the club fell, I leapt toward them, dragging Maggie with me a few steps before she let me go. My right shoulder popped out of joint with a tearing crunch but it didn't stop me. Momentum took over and I crashed into Ash, sending us both to the ground as the club whipped over us. Match let out a roar and I scrambled to stand upright, whimpering as my shoulder socket twisted again.

The other Enders seemed surprised. As if they couldn't believe we'd fight back. "Ready to run?" I asked, as I tried to think past the throbbing ache in my shoulder. I backed away from the Enders, pushing Ash with me. If we could get moving, we had a chance at outrunning them.

"Your father said we should go with them without a fight—"

"And you think that's a good idea?"

Ash didn't answer and I knew I was right, we both did. My father was not in his right mind; he hadn't been for a long time. And until the mental wounds Cassava inflicted on him healed, we couldn't trust him.

We truly were on our own.

A slow building anger started in my belly and spread outward to my hands where the iron manacles clamped my wrists. I fed the power of the earth inherent to me into the iron, pulling the ore apart, molecule by molecule, until they fell to the ground at my feet.

Maggie stared at me and the curl of red lines, indicators of her power climbing her hand, was the only warning I had that she was about to blast us with her element. Fire danced from her hands and onto the ground around us creating a perfect circle. I flicked my hand and the earth covered the fire, putting it out as easily as breathing.

At least easy enough when I was angry and I could reach my power. Without anger backing me, I couldn't tap into the earth and the power within it. A flaw I didn't know how to change.

"Maybe in the Pit you rule, *Maggie*. But not here." She glared at me, and I backed away, bumping into Ash. Except it wasn't Ash.

It was another Ender from the Pit, one I didn't know. He dug his hand into my busted up shoulder, his fingers scooping into the open joint. I screamed, unable to stop the sound from escaping me anymore than I could stop myself from dropping to my knees. The world swayed as the Ender put more pressure on the joint. The sounds of people yelling, and the rush of bodies around us was about all I could make out.

There was a flash of green and gold and suddenly Fern, my father's current wife, stood in front of me trying to stop Maggie and the other Enders from the Pit. Her belly swelled with what would be a younger sibling for me, but even so, she fought for us.

"I am the queen here and I forbid you taking my Enders!" she snapped, pointing at Maggie.

Goddess love her, she was trying. Another voice rose in defiance and I could hardly understand what I was seeing.

Coal stood next to Fern, his back to me but I would know him anywhere. My on-again-and-currently-off-again lover whose hand I'd been forced to cut off in order for him to survive the catastrophe that was the lung burrowers. The last I'd spoken with him, he'd gone more than a little crazy. Something that happened often to those elementals who lost a body part.

Yet there he was, fighting for me. He put his remaining hand on Match's chest and shoved. "She's mine. No one is taking her from me." Well, there went the warm and fuzzies.

I looked around again, now no stars dancing in front of my eyes. Ash was flat on the ground, his face pressed into the dirt. He wasn't fighting back though and I knew I couldn't get us both out of this mess on my own. The pain had overridden the anger and I couldn't reach my connection to the earth any longer.

The Ender holding me down squeezed again and I rolled my head back to stare up at him. His red hair was lighter than the others' from the Pit, almost a blond if not for the distinct red undertones. "Think you can ease up?"

He grinned at me and I was reminded of Eel, an Undine I'd faced in the Deep who had a penchant for hurting people. "Nah, I like you on your knees in front of me, little Terraling. You look good down there."

I tried to pull away but he bore down and the world darkened for a moment as the pain consumed my consciousness.

There was screaming and yelling and I struggled to lift my head because even that movement tweaked the tendons and ligaments I'd torn. Coal picked up Fern and carried her out of the way. His eyes met mine in a brief flash of green. "I'm sorry, Lark. I can't save you."

I let out a breath. "You never could. This isn't anything new."

His face hardened, and behind me, the Ender laughed. "Oh, a spunky one. I hope your trial goes for weeks. You know, I'm one of the guards from the dungeons. I'll be taking care of you. Personally."

How was I not surprised?

Things seemed to slow for a moment, and the sound of my heart hammered in my ears as the leather clad Enders parted. My father walked toward us, but I had no hope in him saving us. I'd lost faith in him a long time ago.

"I wish to have a word with my Enders before they go to their punishment," he said, his normally rich voice holding a distinct tremor to it. Maggie grunted.

"If you try to free them, we will not stand for it."

He waved her off as if she were a buzzing gnat, and stopped in front of me. Slowly he dropped to a crouch so we were eye to eye.

"Your Majesty." I bowed my head.

"Ender Larkspur. I have tried to save you from yourself, but you seem inclined to find trouble wherever you go." Around us, the Enders shifted their feet, and one even laughed.

My father drew a breath and the sound of the air in his lungs was a wet rattle. "The mother goddess has commanded you face your destiny in the Pit without interference from me. She has a task for you there, a life to save."

I raised my head and really looked at him as the finality of his words settled on me. His skin was pale under the perpetual tan and his eyes seemed fogged over; even his clothes hung on his frame. My heart lurched. Had one of the lung burrowers somehow been missed?

As softly as I could, I spoke. "Are you ill?"

He bowed his head so our foreheads touched and his words were for my ears alone. "I believe I am dying, Larkspur. There is no cure in this world for what ails me. I do not know why Fiametta sent her Enders for you, as she swore she held no grudge against you or Ash."

He lifted a trembling hand and cupped the back of my head, holding us tightly together. "Child, be strong, and know that I sorrow for the wrongs done to you, for the first time I see them clearly. I am grateful this illness has come upon me; the fever has wiped away the lies Cassava built in my mind. I will see you when we both walk the far side of the Veil, though I will pray you will not make that journey for a thousand years."

Throat tightening, I couldn't speak past the growing lump. Tears tracked my cheeks as he stood and made his way to Ash.

"You have one duty left to you, Ender." He touched Ash on the shoulder. "You know what it is."

Ash's jaw ticked and he gave a slow nod. "It will be done."

The king's hand fell from Ash's shoulder and Fern ran to him. "You have to stop them."

He didn't stop walking, but his words reached me still. "I have done all I can. They must face this alone."

The Enders closed ranks as my father disappeared, Fern clutching at him and Coal following. If nothing else, I would at least be able to say they tried to save us.

Ash lurched forward, and the Enders all focused on him as he grappled with Match. The Ender behind me did nothing but drive his fingers deeper into my shoulder socket.

"You aren't going anywhere, Terraling. At least, not anywhere you want to be."

The scuffle in front of us died down and the Ender's hand on me tightened right before a flash of black caught the corner of my eye and a club smashed into my skull sending me into oblivion.

The queen's chamber was dark, but that didn't matter. The person whose memories I saw was able to move around with an easy stealth, avoiding the furniture and knickknacks that would give his—and I was sure it was a man's memories I saw—movements away.

"Damn, woman," he growled, "where the hell did you hide it?"

He scoured the room that I could only see in glimpses. It was built in the shape of an octagon, the sides a smooth black stone reminiscent of the clubs the Enders from the Pit used. A bed lay in the middle of the room, spires of black rock curling upward as the four posts and a sheer material that sparkled even in the darkness, draped between them, woven like a spider's web. If I could have shivered, I would have but trapped in someone else's memories left me no ability to move.

"Here we go," he bent near the bed and moved as if to shimmy under it when the sound of sheets sliding about snapped his head up. Peering over the edge of the bed, he stared at his queen. Her red hair was the color of fresh blood, which only accentuated the pale creamy tones of her skin and the deep blue of her eyes. An unusual color in the fire elemental bloodlines. She sat up, the sheet slipping down and pooling around her waist, baring her breasts to the warm air.

"What are you doing in my chambers, Ender?"

He swallowed. "My queen, I wish only to serve you." She could fry his ass in an instant and they both knew it. Her ability with lava was unheard of in all the records of their people. For her, the lava was alive, like a beast she'd tamed and would do her bidding even so far as to defy the laws of nature.

There was only one way he might be able to get out of this alive. As renowned as her ability with the lava was her insatiable libido. "I would serve you in whatever manner you desire of me." His voice turned husky and he made a bold move, sliding his hand across the sheets to brush his fingers against her bare *skin. The top of his hand was scarred, an old wound that hadn't healed cleanly. Four jagged lines that drew down from between his fingers to the base of his wrist.*

She arched an eyebrow. "Whatever manner I desire?"

He bowed his head, breathing in the smell of her sheets, wondering if it would be the last thing he ever saw. "My queen, I am yours to command."

Her fingers dug into his hair and pulled him toward her. "Then pleasure me, Ender. For it has been years since a man was bold enough to brave my chamber without an invitation."

He dipped his head taking her mouth in his own as he pressed her to the bed. So he hadn't found what he was looking for, and his mentor would not be happy, but this was better. With easy access to the queen's chamber, he wouldn't be forced to sneak around. He could get all the information his mentor needed, and together they would take Fiametta down. If he got to ride the queen before she was toppled, all the better. She'd never suspect him.

Slipping out of his black leathers he slid under the covers with the queen, his mouth and hands everywhere bringing her to her peak in a matter of minutes—

I let out a groan as I slipped out of the memory, the lingering lust the memories stirred clinging to me. As a half-breed, the child of Spirit side allowed me to see into other people's memories when we Traveled together. So even though the memory wasn't a surprise, I still was left disoriented.

A quick glance around showed that except for Ash, Match, and one other Ender who was a woman, we were alone. Whoever's memories I'd seen had already left the Traveling room so I had no clue who he was.

Undertones of perfumed cherry blossoms tugged at me and I slowly sat up. Back in the Traveling room in the Pit was not a place I had ever wanted to be again. The walls were rounded, as if we sat inside of the world and looked out from the center. If only I could get my hands on a single armband, I'd be able to get both Ash and me out. I glanced around the room, but there wasn't a band to be had. Damn it.

"They've been moved since the last time you were here, Terraling." The nearly blond Ender swung through the doors and into the room. "So don't think you'll be getting one and skipping out. You have an appointment to keep."

An appointment. Nice way of saying I had an execution hanging over my head and Ash's. And that didn't even take into account my shoulder that was pulled apart, or the memories of what I suspected where a traitor to Fiametta swimming around my head.

Chapter 2

atch pushed Ash ahead of me through the maze that was the Pit. My new friend who seemed to like causing me pain dragged me along behind.

A few minutes in, I had enough energy, and the pain had subsided to a dull throb, allowing me to finally speak. "Do you have a name?"

"Brand." He jabbed a fist into my lower back, shoving me forward and effectively cutting me off from asking him another question. Which was going to be where had Maggie gone? Not that I thought she'd be any kinder but I was curious as to why she'd left us.

The Pit was set up like a beehive and with more hallways and doors than actual rooms. Some of the doors opened straight into the Pit itself, a bubbling pool of lava that to anyone not a fire elemental was instant death. At least, that was what I understood. I'd never seen the actual Pit myself, only heard the rumors. For all I knew it could be the size of a mud puddle. Though I doubted that very much.

I tried to pay attention to the number of turns and twists but it was quickly apparent we were deliberately taken on the longest route possible, and I was sure we backtracked at least twice before we stopped in front of what I assumed was our destination.

The doors were each ten feet across and at least that high. Built out of solid gold, there was a perfect likeness of a wingless serpentine dragon etched into the malleable material. Emeralds for eyes, sapphire scales, and the flame that curled out his mouth was shards of rubies and yellow diamonds. Above the dragon was an inscription:

All who enter shall be judged, and those found lacking shall be destroyed.

"Wow, that's comforting." I couldn't help the sarcasm dripping from my mouth, it covered the fear that grew in my heart. Ash shifted so he was next to me, our Enders flanking either side of us.

"Trust me, Lark. You have to trust me." His voice was low, and his hand reached out to brush my fingers. "Can you do that?"

"Enough talking." Match snapped his club out and drummed the door three times. I looked around while we waited. Behind us were two hulking statues, one of the queen wearing a long dress that billowed out behind her, and next to her was a black panther, sleek and snarling. If I were to guess, I would say the panther was her familiar.

An answering drumbeat echoed from the other side of the doors. Slowly the golden doors swung inward, cutting the dragon in half. The room was coated in gold, from the floor to the walls to the ceilings. Embedded in the gold was every jewel and precious stone I knew and a few I'd only heard of: diamonds, rubies, emeralds, sapphires, amethyst, opals, citrine, malachite, pearls, and so many more scattered about, like they were worth nothing.

The effect was overwhelming, which I was quite sure was the point. Keeping my chin up despite my shoulder, I walked forward with Ash on my left.

In the throne ahead sat the woman from the memory I'd seen. Her likeness to the statue outside the doors was impressive.

Fiametta. Her hair was bound up on her head in a complicated braid that wove in and out of her crown made of rubies held together by thin strands of gold. Simple in its design, it almost disappeared into the deep red of her hair. Her blue eyes didn't flicker, didn't give away even a hint of emotion. She was dressed in black Ender leathers, which surprised me. Was that where she'd started her life? Had she been a princess who'd trained with Enders?

Like me?

Where the hell had that thought come from? No matter how much my blood may have been royal, I would never really be a princess.

A variety of people filled chairs around the edges of the room. I saw the crown prince, Flint, with his distinctive black streak running through the middle of his bright red hair. He'd flirted with Belladonna, my older sister, when she'd been here. His eyes roved over me and a slow smile spread on his lips.

Not a chance in hell, I glared at him.

Two other younger children—probably royalty, by the way they glared at us--also had the distinctive black streak through their red hair.

Cactus, my childhood friend and confidant, a half-breed like myself, stood against one wall, watching us come in. His eyes met mine and I thought for a moment he tried to say something to me in that look. Perhaps goodbye.

Fiametta slowly stood, her body moving with a predatory grace not unlike the black panther at her side. Her familiar let out a jaw cracking yawn and stood with her, its blue eyes as unusual as hers narrowing slightly as it took us in.

"Fiametta, these two will be trouble. You should kill them quickly," the large predator said.

"Be quiet," Fiametta said. "I did not ask your opinion."

The panther's teeth snapped shut and it sat. If I didn't know better, I'd say he was pissed.

For just a moment, I thought I saw a glimmer of pink waver around the queen's head. I blinked. Ash stepped forward, blocking my view of Fiametta. "Your majesty, there has been a misunderstanding."

Fiametta let out a long low laugh as she stepped down the final few steps so she was on even ground with us. "Truly? I doubt that very much, Ender."

"If I could speak with you, I could explain what happened," he said softly, his blond head bowed in submission. She strode forward, her body lithe and lean, except for her bust, which seemed about ready to pop out of the skintight leathers. Her hand snaked out and she grabbed Ash's hair at the back of his head jerking his face upright. "Whatever you have to say, do it now, or I will throw you into the Pit and be done with you."

I couldn't see his face, couldn't tell what was going through his mind. Like everyone else in the room, I waited, wondering what the hell he could possibly say that would pull our asses from the fire in the most literal of senses.

Ash slowly spoke, "Your majesty—"

"Cut the worm shit, Ender. Spit out whatever you have

to say," Fiametta said, her voice as cold as the lava flows were hot.

"I am responsible for the four deaths of your Enders. My companion Ender Larkspur did not wield the blade for any of them."

Before I could open my mouth to deny Ash's words, Brand slammed his hand over my lips and whispered in my ear. "Don't make his sacrifice for nothing."

Fiametta's eyes slid from Ash to me. "Ender Brand. Let her speak."

Brand's one hand found my shoulder again and dug into it. Damn it, how far back had Ash set this up? I thought about him finding me in the forest, how his kiss had felt like a goodbye.

He'd known they were coming for us, and he'd planned this all along. There was no other explanation.

With my mouth clear of Brand's hand, I took a deep breath, knowing what Brand said was true. If I claimed the deaths as my own, I would damn both Ash and myself to swim in the Pit. But if I were still free, maybe I could find a way out for both of us. A slim chance, but more than we'd had before. "You have to give him a trial."

Fiametta arched an eyebrow at me. "I have to do no such thing. He is not of royal blood, and there are witnesses who wish to see him pay for his sins."

Ash slid in front of me again. "No, I confess to it all. You don't have to bring the witnesses in."

Brand held me back as Match pulled Ash away from me. "Hold still, girl."

I didn't even realize I was struggling until Brand spoke. I tried again to get loose from him. "You can't do this!"

Fiametta let out a long low laugh. "You believe my Enders' lives are not worth repercussion? That their lives are worth less than his? I think not, Terraling." Her eyes blazed.

"I lost four Enders. FOUR lives were taken, girl. It is a small penance to pay that he—" she grabbed Ash by the jaw and twisted him around to face me—"pays with his own life. As Enders you are held to higher standards. You of all people should know that. Be glad I do not toss you into the Pit alongside him."

Horror and guilt flooded me. I was the guilty party and Fiametta was right—there had to be penance for those lives lost. Not by Ash, but by me.

Brand held me and I realized he'd softened his grip on me, steadying me more than holding. "How long?" I whispered the words and for just a moment I thought I saw a flicker of compassion in Fiametta's eyes.

"Three days. As the sun rises on the third day the lava will be at its hottest peak in nearly three hundred years. Rather fitting for the first execution of an outsider, don't you think? He will walk into the Pit, or be thrown, if need be," she said. "And you will be kept in the dungeons. The last thing I need is you causing more trouble."

Brand cleared his throat. "My queen. I would like to personally offer to watch over her. My wife could use *help* of a big strong girl like the Terraling."

Help? He was asking to use me as a slave while I was here. Slavery was something strictly forbidden by the mother goddess . . . yet I'd seen the rule circumvented in the Deep too.

Fiametta tipped her head to one side. "Brand, that is a great task. I do not wish to put your family in harm's way."

He gave me a light shake. "I'll throw her in the Pit myself if she puts one foot outside the lines."

The queen of the Pit smiled softly and pleasure lit her face. "So be it. Let the Terraling work for her time here, and let her watch her companion die."

Brand tossed me over his shoulder. "Come, my wife needs laundry hand scrubbed."

His words were so mundane, so simple that they jarred my brain into action.

"No! Ash, don't do this. ASH!" I hadn't meant to scream, and yet, I felt like he was being taken from me and if nothing else, I knew he was meant to be in my life.

"Lark. Please trust me." Was all he was able to say before he was slammed to the ground, his face pressed against the golden floor, his eyes only a shade lighter than the precious metal as he stared at me.

Sick to my stomach, I knew it was my fault he was going to be executed in my place. That was what my father meant when he spoke to Ash. This was his final job, his final duty. To keep me out of the fire. But it was my reckless behavior and decisions that brought us to this point. I had to do something.

Brand packed me out the monstrous double doors, past the statue of Fiametta and her familiar, and to the left of the throne room. We'd only gone a few hundred feet when he put me down. "I'll take you to the healers."

I wanted to jerk away from him, pull a weapon and run after Ash. I wanted to break out of the Pit like we'd done before and thumb my nose at them, prove that as earth elementals we were just as strong. Except I couldn't. I had no weapons and my shoulder was swollen to the size of a small watermelon. Getting my joint back into place was going to be like jamming an elephant into a keyhole. "Why are you doing this?"

Brand put a hand on the back of my neck and shoved me forward. "Move."

"Tell me what the hell is going on!" I yelled and he slammed me forward, my face and body pressed against the wall, his knee jammed into my lower back.

"So impetuous. I see why he had problems training you." His mouth dropped to my ear and his whisper was harsh against my skin. "Ash is taking the rap because he couldn't protect your mother and little brother years ago. He's paying the penance for their lives, Larkspur. And I'm helping him because he's my friend and I trust him when he says you are more important than any of us realize." He eased off me and I slowly turned. His eyes were serious and no longer the lecherous leer he put on before. It had all been an act.

"He said all that?" I put a hand to my head. "Brand, those Enders wanted to kill us. We had to fight or we would have died."

He nodded, his orange eyes narrowed under lowered brows. "I know. We have a problem in our ranks. Which is the other reason I'm helping you. Come, the first thing is taking care of your arm. Then we can discuss how we're going to clear out the snakes in our nest."

Brand waved me ahead of him and I carefully walked where he wanted. The things Brand said swirled in my head and I struggled to think straight around the pain radiating from my shoulder. The rod of Asclepius floated into view. A snake wrapped around a rod embedded into the door: the mark of the healer's rooms. My vision blurred and the snake seemed to move as I fell under the tightening net of pain that drove deep into my body, and my legs buckled.

Chapter 3

I lay flat on my back for the second time that day, staring at the ceiling while Smit, one of the Pit's healers, worked on my arm. He'd helped me before, when Ash and I had broken into the Pit. His hands were gentle as he manipulated my arm. "I'm going to force it back into the joint, and there are no two ways about this. It's going to hurt."

I must have nodded because he looked away from me for a second and then Brand was holding me down. My mind raced with possibilities of how I was going to get both me and Ash out of the Pit. Most pressing was how in the name of the mother goddess was I going to pull Ash out of the fire he'd flung himself into. Smit lifted my hand and I drew in a slow breath. With a twist and a hard push, he forced my shoulder back into joint. There was a click and a slight crunch, then a soft pop as the ball slid back into the socket.

For a split second I thought it wasn't so bad, but the pain was slow in coming and when it hit I was glad Brand's hands held me down. I writhed under the pain, the wave of adrenaline, relief, and feeling of sharp knives all jabbed into me and was too much to contain. Biting down on a cry, I slowly relaxed as my body eased to the bed once more.

Brand patted me on my good shoulder. "Now we're ready to go."

I sat up and the world spun. I thought I saw a flicker of gray and white fur.

Smit let out a laugh. "What are you doing here, Peta? I thought the queen had you banished."

Blinking, I stared down at my feet into the bright green eyes of Peta in her house cat form. When she wanted to, she could shift into a snow leopard. As a familiar, she was supposed to protect and watch over the powerful elemental she was assigned to. In her case, the last Salamander she'd protected died in the Deep. Which was where I'd met her.

But she saved my ass twice and I wouldn't forget that, or show her disrespect in any way. "Hello, Peta." I slid to the side of my bed leaving room for her to leap up. Her green eyes didn't blink even once.

"Dirt Girl. I see you're in trouble again."

Brand grunted. "Cat, you're pretty damn mouthy for one on the edge of being booted out."

Peta let out a sneeze that could have been a snort, and wiped a paw over her face. "Please. Just because I've always been assigned to idiots is not my fault."

I dropped my feet to the floor. "Good luck with your next fire assignment then. I hope they are smarter than your last."

Brand tipped his head to the left and walked away, I

followed. Or would have. A tiny set of claws dug into my lower leg. I stopped and once more looked down. "What do you want, cat?"

Those glittering green eyes narrowed as she let go of me.

"Dirt Girl, I'm going to need that luck. The mother goddess has given me my new assignment already and I don't like it."

I threw my one good arm into the air. "Wonderful. Good luck. I have to go, things to do." With that I strode away. What the hell did the cat want anyway? There was nothing I could do about her assignment no matter how bad it was. Damn, unless she was spying on me for her new master. I looked over my shoulder, but didn't see her.

Following Brand through the twists and turns of the Pit, I was surprised where he took me. The hallway opened and overlooked a cavern whose ceiling rose hundreds of feet above our heads. From where we stood, I could have jumped to the floor easily. But it wasn't the height that caught my eye, or even the sheer size of at least thirty acres hidden within the mountain.

Around the edges of the cavern, homes snuggled into the rock walls, and out front in tiny boxed gardens plants struggled to survive. Children played and women laughed as they went about their daily routines. The sounds of music and singing floated in the air. A true village filled with Salamanders carrying on life.

Through the village, a river of lava flowed, gurgling like a brook, heat bubbles erupting here and there. Even at the distance I was, the heat felt unreal. As soon as sweat popped out on my skin, it began to dry.

A child, a little girl with pigtails and pale pink dress, ran for the edge of the lava flow and I couldn't help but suck in a sharp breath. She would be burned to a crisp if someone didn't stop her. I took a step and Brand grabbed me as he chuckled. I whipped my head around to stare at him. "How can you laugh?"

"Just watch, Terraling."

I spun back to see the child dip her hands into the molten mass and hold it up . . . giggling while she did so. Two more scoops and she moved the small amount of lava to a hole she dug and poured it in. Mother goddess, she was playing in it.

I swallowed hard. It was one thing to know Salamanders dealt with the fire, but another to see a child play in an active lava flow.

"Come, meet my family." Brand started down a set of steps cut into the mountain that led us on a switchback path to the floor. A soft meow snapped my head around as we reached the bottom. Peta stood at the top of the stairs.

Brand snorted. "We don't need you following us, bad luck cat."

She didn't answer, just leapt from the stair to my shoulders where she landed easily and I fought not to crumple under her tiny weight, my bad shoulder reminding me it needed time to heal.

Peta balanced there, her tiny feet somehow impossibly heavy on my tender shoulder. "I told you I had a new assignment." Her eyes stared into mine, glittering with her obvious distaste and the realization of what she said slammed into me.

I lifted my hands as I sputtered. "No, you're kidding me right? I don't need a familiar."

But as I said it, I knew I was wrong. A familiar was the one soul I could depend on, the one soul that would have my back no matter what. But . . . "Peta, you must be mistaken, you're meant for a Salamander. Not . . . me."

She draped herself across my shoulders and the warmth of her body eased the ache in my injured shoulder. Her tail tickled down the front of my neck as it twitched. "I didn't ask for this. If you have a complaint, get in line to take it up with the mother goddess."

I turned to see Brand staring at us with wide eyes. "I'd get in line. That cat has lost more of her charges than any familiar in the Pit. Seriously, that cat is bad luck."

Peta gave a barely felt shiver and I lifted a hand to her, putting one palm against the silken fur along her back. A simple choice lay in front of me. If Peta truly was my familiar, I didn't want to have the kind of relationship she'd had with Loam, her previous charge. I wanted to have her on my side, a friend and confidant.

I lowered my hand. "She saved me twice already, Brand. If the mother goddess feels I am deserving of her then I am grateful."

The twitching of her tail eased and she let out a soft breath against my neck but said nothing more. I took a step, feeling the change in my balance with her along for the ride. Three steps and I had it, walking as normally as if I'd always had a cat riding on my shoulders.

Brand arched an eyebrow and then shrugged. "It's your life, but I'll tell you now that my wife won't be happy to have her in the house."

My jaw tightened but I kept my mouth shut. I would need help to get Ash out alive and that meant for the moment I needed to keep Brand happy. As an Ender, he would have access to weapons and understood the layout of the Pit. My mind worked all the possible details, but the whole of it came to a simple piece. I had to find the armbands used for Traveling, steal them, and then break into the dungeon to get Ash. From there, we would get to the Traveling room.

A walk in the park on a sunny morning couldn't be easier. And maybe if I told myself that enough, I'd believe it.

Brand led the way to a bridge that arched high over the lava, but even with that distance the heat was intense and my skin tightened as the moisture was quickly sucked out of me. I hurried across, passing Brand and not caring that he grinned at me. "Too much?"

A quick nod was all I gave him. Suddenly going back to the Deep for a swim in the Caribbean waters wasn't looking too bad. If you discounted the sharks, Kracken, crocodiles, and tsunamis. On the far side of the bridge stood a large statue carved out of an opalescent white stone I didn't recognize. The creature, a sinuous dragon, reached at least three times my height. I put a hand to it. "What is this?"

Brand stopped a few feet ahead of me. "A symbol of our world."

"No, I meant the stone."

"Don't know, no one does. The statue has been there as long as Salamanders have existed in this mountain."

He walked on.

"Guess that means this conversation is done," I mumbled. Peta snorted.

We passed several homes and all activity slowly stopped. The women stood and stared at me, not bothering to hide the distrust, and in several cases, outright hate in their strange orange eyes.

"Be wary, Dirt Girl. You killed four men and these women know it," Peta said.

I tried to swallow past the guilt rising in me. "Were they married?"

"One of them was," Brand said, "He had a child on the way."

Absolute sorrow washed through me and I stopped where I was, struggling to breathe. Those deaths had been necessary to save my family, but knowing I'd stolen a father from his unborn child? That was not who I was, I would never willingly hurt someone like that.

And yet I had done it without a thought. Without a care of who else I might affect as my spear thrust forward. "Mother goddess." I leaned forward, putting my hands onto my thighs as the truth settled on me like a weight. I should be the one in the dungeon, awaiting my execution.

Peta butted her head against my ear, gaining my attention. "You do what you must to survive. We all do, Dirt Girl. That you feel their loss . . . that is good. When you stop feeling the pain of your actions . . .that is when you must be afraid. When you no longer care if you kill, then we have a problem."

Slowly I straightened. "Take me to her."

Brand shook his head. "No. She is crazed with her loss."

Anger kissed at my heels and I used it to tap into my element. Pulling on the earth was easy here, deep in the mountain. The rock around me rumbled, and the women approaching backed away. I lifted a hand and touched one of Peta's front paws. "Peta. Do you know where she is?"

"Brand is right. Now is not the time. Later perhaps."

I let out a slow breath, thinking about the little I knew of familiars. My training was sparse, but I did recall my father pointing out that his two familiars were to act as guides when he needed them. A voice of reason. Which explained why he'd sent them away when Cassava was in charge.

A second breath escaped me. "All right, Peta."

She startled on her perch. "You're listening to me?"

I shrugged, immediately regretting the movement. With a pained grimace, I stood next to Brand. "That is part of your job, isn't it? To advise me?"

"Yes, but . . . rarely does anyone abide by their familiars. It's why so few of us are connected to elementals now. Even the queen discounts Jag." Her teeth clicked shut on the last word like she'd said more than she'd planned. Jag, that must have been the panther at the queen's side.

We were quiet as Brand led the rest of the way to his home. On the exterior, it looked like all the other homes, bare, sparsely carved, set deep into the wall, and a scraggly garden with only a few shoots of green. But when we stepped through the doorway, the room was alight with a fire burning in the large hearth directly across from us (which I hoped was for cooking and not additional warmth) and light coming from the ceiling. I stared up at the light, trying to understand how it was possible.

"Light tubes, they bounce the sunlight down to us, and it's how we grow our fruits and vegetables, as meager as they are," a soft, whispery voice said. I lowered my eyes from the tube to see a woman who matched the tones of her words. Her body was narrow and looked more like that of a Sylph's with her almost frail bone structure. Most Salamanders were solid of build, not unlike my family. But she was almost petite. Of course, her bright red hair a shade that resembled a tulip marked her for her bloodline. That and her pale yellow eyes. Not gold like Ash's, but a true yellow, like a cat's.

She held out her hand, palm up. "My name is Smoke."

"Put your hand over hers, palm down," Peta whispered in my ear.

I did as told, my palm brushing against Smoke's. "I'm Lark."

Brand grunted. "She knows who you are."

Smoke pulled her hand back. "Are you hungry? I imagine after your journey you might be." Her eyes flicked to Peta, but she said nothing.

"Thank you, yes." The whole conversation felt false, like we said things only to cover the empty space, to keep the silence from creeping in. But why?

A pounding of feet on rock spun me around and my

hands went to my waist for a spear not there. Three boys ran into the eating area from deeper within the home. Each of them had Smoke's bright red hair, but they were built like their father and they all had his eyes. They stopped as a unit, staring at me.

"Wow, she's really pretty," the smallest of the three boys said, and I liked him immediately. Peta snorted softly.

"Typical male."

Brand dropped a hand on the largest of the three boys who almost matched him in size despite the fact he was obviously not fully grown, his arms and legs gangly. "These are our boys. Stryker, Cano, and Tinder. They were supposed to be out of the house for the day, but it looks as though they heard their mother say something about food."

The smallest boy who'd said I was pretty, Tinder, looked up at his father. "We just wanted to see her. We've never met a Terraling. And why has she got one of our cats with her?"

Peta yawned wide enough that her tiny jaws cracked. "Because no one else could look after her."

The boys nodded as if what Peta said made perfect sense, and then they scooted outside, their mother shouting after them. "Stryker don't let Tinder near the flows or the Pit! No swimming today!"

Brand glanced at his wife. "Why can't they go to the Pit?"

Her brow furrowed. "I just do not want them going. I have a bad feeling about the Pit right now."

Brand nodded, obviously trusting his wife's intuition. I looked at Peta but she wouldn't meet my gaze.

"Listen to your mother. No swimming!" Brand said.

There was a chorus of groans from the three boys, and then silence. Brand let out a slow breath. "Sit down, Lark."

I sat, though I perched on the edge of the chair. "I'm not leaving without him, Brand. You can either help me find a way to free him, or I will find it on my own."

Brand looked from his wife to me. "Three days isn't enough time in the world to come up with a defense for an Ender who has admitted to a crime, and you must do that while looking as though you are helping Smoke. That is your only cover while you are here."

Drawing in a deep breath, I reluctantly nodded. "I know, but I think I have someone who can help, someone who knows the ins and outs of the Pit."

The only question was, would Cactus be willing to help me again? Or would he, once more, find his allegiance with this side of his bloodline?

Brand looked to his wife. "I know about your friend. Cactus barely escaped punishment for the help he gave you the last time you were here. But even if he won't help you, I will. Ash spoke highly of you, of your sense of justice. We need your help, Terraling. Our queen does not see the danger around her and we are all bound to her, unable to make her see."

"You think I would help her? When she threatens to kill my friend? Without even a trial?" The question popped out of me before I could stop it.

A snort escaped the Ender as he leaned back in his chair. "For justice, I think you will. If Ash is right about you that is. He told me about you and Queen Finley, how you saved her from the usurper in the Deep. Would you truly leave someone you could help behind?"

If Ash was right about me. The words echoed in my brain. I wasn't sure I was willing to help, not after the Deep. And Finley was a little girl, no matter how much power she had within her, she'd *needed* someone to help her. Fiametta was a full-grown bitch.

But Brand wouldn't help me rescue Ash if I said no to his request.

"All right, I will help," I said, the lie hard on my tongue.

Peta tightened her claws into me and I couldn't look at her, afraid she would see the dishonesty.

She laid her head down on my shoulder. "Dirt Girl, you are going to get us both killed."

Chapter 4

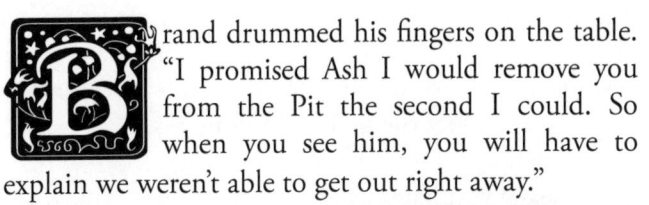

Brand drummed his fingers on the table. "I promised Ash I would remove you from the Pit the second I could. So when you see him, you will have to explain we weren't able to get out right away."

"You want me to lie to him," I said, leaning back in my seat and crossing my arms. Peta snorted and I fought not to cringe. Only moments before I'd lied to Brand and now I was calling him out for the same thing.

Smoke pushed a platter of food in front of me. "Eat, then we can discuss this once you have a full belly."

With a grunt, Brand dug into the food and I followed his lead, trusting that Peta would say something if I broke some sort of taboo.

The food was nothing short of amazing. Sticky rice

covered in a thick, spicy sauce alongside chunks of mango and pork was spooned onto my plate. Within two bites, sweat broke out on my brow, but it was good, the warmth filling me. I ate three plates' worth before pushing it away and reaching for a pewter cup of what I thought was water. I had two gulps before my tongue registered milk, with ice cubes clinking in it to add to the chill.

"It will soothe the fire in your mouth." Smoke smiled, her lips curling up at the edges only a little.

"Thank you." I took another gulp and held the cup up to Peta, tipping it so she could reach the milk. She paused and stared at me a moment before she stuck her head in and lapped it up. Brand stopped eating, his mouth hanging open and his fork halfway to his mouth.

I looked from him to Smoke. "What?"

She dropped her eyes, that small smile ghosting across her lips.

"Nothing." He shook his head several times and went back to eating. What the hell had I done now?

Smoke let out a soft breath. "Sharing food with your familiar means you have accepted her as your own. It is surprising, that is all. How long has it been, Peta, since your charge actually accepted you?"

Peta pulled her head out, milk clinging to her whiskers in tiny white droplets. "That is enough for me, Dirt Girl." She didn't answer Smoke's question. Though I was curious about Peta's past charges, it wasn't high on my priority list.

I tipped the cup and drank the last of the milk, my argument ready. "Brand, if you are truly Ash's friend, you know he didn't kill those Enders. You know he doesn't deserve to die for a perceived mistake that happened years ago. It wasn't his fault my mother and brother were killed on his watch. That was all Cassava's doing. He's a good man and this is wrong on all levels."

A low grumbling breath escaped the Ender across from me. "Those things are true, but I am tied to this family which is why I need you to help me, I cannot go against Fiametta's wishes any more than you can go against your king's."

"That's ridiculous, you aren't a slave," I snapped. "You're just using that for an excuse not to do what's right."

Brand leaned forward, one eyebrow raised high enough that it nearly touched his hairline. "Have you not gone through your trial with the mother goddess? You must have if you are an Ender."

I frowned. "Of course I have. What has that to do with this?"

He placed his broad hands on the table. "Then you swore to uphold your family in all things, swore your life to them, and to obey your king no matter what he would ask of you."

Well, worm shit and green sticks, what did I say to that? I had sworn nothing of the kind. The mother goddess had helped me past the block Cassava placed on my abilities, and sent me back.

I must have been silent too long.

Peta's claws dug into me. "Dirt Girl."

I cleared my throat and slowly shook my head. "No. The mother goddess didn't have me swear to anyone."

Brand looked at his wife who stared at me. "Then you," she said softly, "are in a very unique position. You are not tied by those bonds all other Enders are. Brand cannot help you, which is exactly why he needs you. But I can. I am no Ender and have no unbreakable bonds."

Brand grunted as if she'd kicked him in the balls. "Smoke, we've discussed this already. I don't want you getting tangled in this. Fiametta is ready to blow, and I don't want her seeing you as an enemy."

Smoke cleared the plates. "Our queen is always on edge.

It is her nature. She is like a mountain perpetually threatening to burst its seams."

I stood, pushing my chair back, questions swirling, one in particular. "Why would you two help me? I've killed four of your Enders." There, I said it out loud.

"Have you? Where are the bodies, Terraling?" Smoke's eyes bore into mine and I saw the keen mind behind the quiet movements and frail bones. "If there are no bodies, how is it proof you killed them?"

In a strange way, she was right. There was no evidence if there were no bodies. But I thought there was more to what she was saying. "What happened to the bodies? Or are you saying they didn't die?" No death would mean no punishment. I would just have to find them.

"I was there, one of Smit's helpers. Those four Enders *are* dead, Lark."

There went that idea.

She continued. "But their bodies were put immediately into the Pit. Without burial."

"Like something was being hidden," Peta said. A shiver slipped up and down my spine and I wriggled my shoulders trying to dissipate the feeling. Those were my thoughts exactly. The only reason to throw bodies into the Pit immediately would be to hide something. Like how they died.

Which made no sense if I was the one who'd caused the deaths, wouldn't they want the evidence preserved?

Smoke wiped her hands on her pants. "Come, let us walk together, we can discuss what must be done first."

Brand stood slowly. "You two be careful. And take the laundry with you or what little cover you have for taking her out will be blown."

That was right, I was supposed to be a *helper* while I was in the Pit. Smoke pointed to a woven basket heaped with clothes. "Lark, take the basket. I will take the rocks."

I scooped up the basket and Peta leapt into it, perched on top like a tiny feline queen. Smoke gathered four smooth, flat rocks shaped perfectly to fit into the hand, used for beating the clothes clean.

She went to her husband and kissed him lightly on his lips. He reached out to her and touched her face, his hands so gentle for their size. I felt as though I was seeing something intimate, and not meant for my eyes as they whispered their goodbyes. "Be careful, my sweet firebrand," he said softly.

We left the home and started across the cavern in silence. Around us, the hum of activity continued as people's lives carried on in the daily grind. But they were happy. I had to give them that. Very different from the atmosphere I'd experienced in the Deep where the Undines had been terrified to even speak, never mind laugh and sing.

The woven basket pressed into my hip, shaping itself to my curve. Peta bobbed along with my steps, her eyes flicking around the cavern. She lifted her head, stretching her neck, her eyes wide.

I looked in the direction she stared. A small figure darted along the wall, paralleling us. Dressed in black from head to toe, it probably stood as high as my shoulder, at most. "Smoke . . ."

She stopped, glanced quickly at the figure and then away, a light shiver running through her. "They have been seen, two cloaked figures darting about the caves and where they go, disaster follows any who interact with them. Avert your eyes, Terraling. You do not want her to notice you."

Smoke put a hand on my arm and tugged me in the opposite direction, but I couldn't help but stare over my shoulder. The dark figure paused at an entranceway and turned back. A low laugh rumbled as the silhouette lifted a hand to me with a jaunty wave.

If it weren't for the heat of the cavern, the cold chill that hit me would have been overwhelming. Something about the way the figure waved, the tilt of the head . . . there was a dark familiarity about them. "Let me guess, that is part of the problem Brand spoke of."

"No, the ghosts have come and gone for years." Smoke directed me toward a set of stairs that took us down to a lower plateau in the cavern. "They are problematic and they bring trouble wherever they go. But they cannot be caught, because they aren't tangible, so there is nothing we can do about them."

Which told me the Salamanders had in fact tried to catch the ghosts and failed. Pride was a funny thing with fire elementals, and I wasn't about to argue that the "ghosts" were probably not ghosts at all. The figure had been too solid, too *real* to be anything as intangible as a specter.

The farther away we got from the main lava flow, the easier the air was to breathe, the less my sweat dried and the cooler I became. Steam rose ahead of us, and the sound of a burbling river pooled in my ears. A sound that almost felt like home.

"Terraling, traitors are in our midst," Smoke said softly, her words barely loud enough to be heard over the water and I realized why she brought me here. Even side-by-side, our words were drowned in the sloshing of water over rocks and the bubble of steam.

Smoke led me to the edge of the river and dropped to her knees. I did the same, so our legs pressed hard against each other. The sand below me cushioned my knees and it was then I noted it wasn't sand but a pale gray ash. Handing Smoke some of the clothes, I took one of the shirts and dunked it in the water, using the rocks and ash to get it clean. A task I'd done a thousand times in my life already, and I fell into it with ease.

"They are trying to bring down our queen. Brand believes it is one of the Enders who is setting this up."

Rolling the cloth in my hands, I pressed it between my knuckles and scrubbed at the stain I'd seen. The water was hot to the point of turning my skin bright pink, and I dunked the shirt into it several times. The memory I'd seen as we Traveled to the Pit was fresh in my mind. But I couldn't just spit out I'd seen the traitor in action.

"I think he's probably right. It would make sense from the angle of getting close to her. Who would benefit from her being killed? Her oldest son?" The answer was obvious to me, Fiametta's son, Flint, would be the heir, no doubt. With her out of the way, he would rule. Open and shut case, why did they need me?

Smoke shook her head. "While he might try to rule, our family has always been led by a test of strength. Fiametta was an Ender when the old queen died. A series of games and challenges were set up by the old queen, and those who wanted to rule had to survive. Fiametta was the last one standing." She paused and splashed the shirt she was washing deep into the water, swirling the ash out of it. "Her son is weak in his power, and in his head. He is too caught up in his own vanity to be of any use to anyone. He knows he will never rule."

She offered me one of the flat rocks and I used it to pound a pair of pants.

There was still something I didn't understand. "What has happened to make you think there is a traitor, though?"

Smoke's head lowered. "The lava flows. They are doing strange things, burning people when they shouldn't. Nothing serious, but you have to understand, Terraling, we *don't burn*. The lava, fire, it is our element. It is our home. And it is turning on us. Fiametta says she has it under control, but Brand has seen her battle the lava. Seen her buckled under its power and close off whole sections of the Pit because she can't stem the flow. And again, there are strange burns. Always it happens around the Pit, as though that is the epicenter."

Peta sat in the now empty basket, her eye peering at me over the edge. "There is more. Something with the night bells has shifted. People are sleeping longer, and are harder to wake up. I have seen that, too."

I opened my mouth to ask her what she meant by that. What did bells have to do with sleep?

Without warning, the ground under my knees heaved upward, throwing me forward, head first into the steaming river. The water tumbled me like the clothes we'd been cleaning, driving me to the bottom of the river where the water was cooler and I wished I had my hooked earring that allowed me to breathe water as if it were air. But I'd lost that in the Deep.

Slowly I was pushed downstream, the rocks at the bottom seemed to hold me to the streambed. No, that *was* what was happening. The rocks were piling on my legs and torso, keeping me under the water; drowning me even as the water shoved me closer to the intersection where the lava flow met the river.

Worm shit didn't begin to describe the trouble I was in. I clawed at the river bottom, digging my heels in to stop my forward momentum. Rocks flipped up and crashed onto me, smashing me in the head, chest and stomach, knocking the wind out of me. I fought not to breathe in the water, to hold what was left of my air as my lungs burned.

I flailed, fighting with everything I had, but the more I fought, the more the earth itself tried to kill me.

Wait. The earth wasn't trying to kill me. A *Terraling* was. Anger snapped through me, allowing me to grab hold of the power of the earth. I pushed it through the rocks, breaking them into sand. With the weight removed, the water slung my body toward the lava flow. Around me, the water heated with each second. I swam hard against the current as I pushed off the bottom.

Breaking through the surface, I gasped in a breath and dared a look behind me. The steady glow of lava and the steaming hiss of the river as it met its brother were far too close.

In the distance, Smoke ran toward me, but she wouldn't make it in time, and I would burn up in a matter of seconds. Would Fiametta let Ash go when I died? I hoped so.

"Dirt Girl, swim to the edge and don't dawdle." Peta snapped me out of my state of near death musing.

I swam toward the shoreline, and was losing more ground to the river, but I knew Peta was right. This was my only chance. She was in her snow leopard form, keeping pace with me on the edge of the riverbank, her round ears pinned back and her eyes narrowed against the steam. The water temperature approached the boiling point. I was slowly cooking, my skin tingling with the near scalding water. I slipped below the water. Peta's green eyes locked on mine.

"I'm sorry," she said. I was dying and she felt bad. Bet I was her shortest lived charge. I wanted to tell her it was okay, that I wasn't really hurting. As a way to die, apparently boiling alive wasn't all that bad. I might have said something along those lines to her, but I wasn't sure. I couldn't feel much of anything.

A fierce, sharp pain sliced into my right hand and a tugging sensation pulled on me. Someone hoisted me out of the water. The pain in my hand eased and then replaced by an even deeper pain in the same place. Like blunted knives driven between the bones in my hand while crunching down on them with a tremendous force.

I screamed then realized Peta had dragged me out of the

water at the last second, first with her claws, and then her teeth. I lay on my back staring at the cavern ceiling, noticing all the light tubes pointed at us, making it daylight deep with the mountain.

"Dirt Girl. If you decide to go swimming, perhaps a less dangerous place would be good, eh?" Peta snapped at me as she paced by my head. "Is it not enough everyone thinks I'm bad luck? To lose you on the first day I'm assigned to you would be the end of my reputation completely. How could I ever show my face again?"

I reached to her with my good hand. "Thanks for saving me. That's three times now. You must like me."

She snorted. "Why did you dive in?"

Easing myself into a sitting position, I put a hand to my head. "I didn't. Someone pushed me."

"No one pushed you. I was right there," she snapped at me again with her words and her teeth.

"A Terraling pushed me, using the ground to unbalance me." I backed away from the river, not wanting a repeat. "And they tried to hold me to the bottom of the river."

Peta stopped pacing. "One of your own?"

I nodded. "You aren't the only bad luck around here, Peta. I'm not well liked within my own family or the Pit."

"Wonderful," she muttered, her body shimmering lightly as she shifted to her housecat form.

My whole body tingled from the heated water, but slowly the discomfort faded, and my skin went from a brilliant shade of pink to its natural tones. Healing as an elemental was usually fast, but I didn't think this was all on me, not when my hand that Peta had bitten was stitching itself back together.

"What are you doing?"

"I'm letting you draw on me. That is what elementals do;

they allow their charges to be stronger, faster, and heal at a speed that keeps them alive. Or is supposed to, anyway."

I frowned. "Well, stop it. I don't want to draw from you."

She frowned at me. "Too good to draw from a cat?"

There wasn't a chance to answer her as Smoke reached us, out of breath. "Why in the world did you jump into the river?"

Peta shook her head slightly and I lowered mine as I cradled my clawed and bitten hand. "I didn't mean to, I stood and then stumbled forward. I'm a klutz, always tripping on things."

I dared a look up. Smoke wasn't buying it, as she placed her hands on her hips. "Did you make eye contact with her?"

I blinked several times as I tried to process who she meant. "Her?"

"The smaller specter. Did you make eye contact with her?"

Shivering, my body cold after being in the superheated water, I nodded. "I did."

"Well, that explains it, then." Smoke held a hand out to me as if the conversation and what had happened was all over. And maybe for her it was.

For me though, her words started a chain reaction in my head. The specter seemed familiar to me, and then a Terraling tried to kill me. Cassava was still in hiding after her failed attempt at taking the throne at the Rim, but could she be here, looking for revenge? Or maybe looking for a way to convince Fiametta to help her? They *were* friends, I knew that, so Cassava being in the Pit in hiding was more than plausible.

Standing, I followed Smoke to the laundry and helped her pile it into the basket.

"That is enough excitement for one day," Smoke said.

Peta snorted. "It's not over yet."

Smoke's body stiffened. "Ah, mother goddess, this is not good."

I looked over her to several women who strode toward us. The one in the lead was very pregnant and had dried tear tracks streaking her cheeks.

My familiar leapt to my shoulder. "That is the wife of one of the Enders you killed."

Heart sinking to my feet, I lowered the basket. I'd caused this pain, no matter the reason behind it.

I let out a slow breath. "Whatever comes of this, I will take."

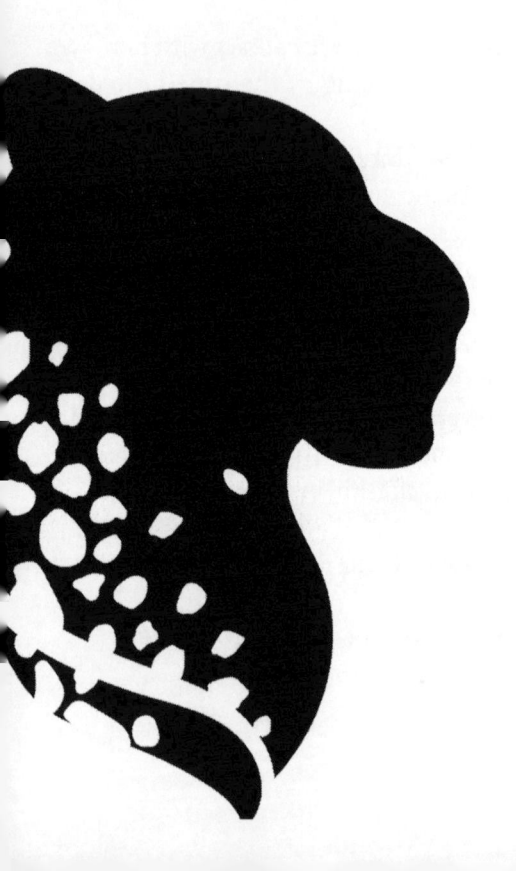

Chapter 5

Smoke tried to stop them, but was pushed aside by the woman in front. "Out of our way, half-breed freak." Smoke stumbled, going to her knees in the soft ash at the edge of the bank, but she wasn't hurt.

I held my ground as the pregnant woman reached me. Her eyes were bloodshot with tears, the pale yellow irises that of a weak flame. It looked as though she'd shorn her hair herself, and I vaguely recalled something Salamanders did when they were grieving.

"You are the Terraling who stabbed my mate?" The words bubbled out of her alongside more tears.

I nodded. "I am."

Her slap was hard, and snapped my head to the side. A second and third slap followed close on its heels, my still aching skin screaming to back away.

But I didn't move. She collapsed forward, surprising me. I caught her and lowered her to the ground as her sobs shook her unwieldy frame. Her hands dug into my arms as she clung to me, her grief overtaking her.

"I'm so sorry," I whispered, the memory of my own losses allowing me to understand how deep the pain would go. How it burrowed into your bones and stole a piece of you that you didn't even know existed. A piece that once gone could never be replaced, but only seen from a distance as other people lived their lives without fear of loss because they'd never experienced it.

"I hate you," she whispered, an echo of my words so many years ago to Cassava.

"I know," I said. Her eyes lifted to mine, spilling with tears and her friends drew her away, their eyes as condemning as any executioners. They helped her stand as she babbled, her words sounding as if she'd said them hundreds of times.

"I saw him in the healer's rooms, I saw him, and he smiled at me and he was fine. They stitched him up, the wound in his side wasn't all that bad. They said he'd be fine, out in the morning. Ready to come home." Her breath hitched and her friends cooed that it was all right. They knew all she said was true. "But they were wrong, the healers were wrong. He wasn't all right. In the morning, he was dead, his wound open as if he'd been stabbed again, the stitches ripped, blood everywhere. Goddess, the blood!" She would have fallen if her friends hadn't had their hands on her.

I ran around, getting in front of the woman. "Wait, stop. You said he was fine. That the wound was healing?"

Her eyes found mine slowly. "Yes. I held his hand, he touched my belly. Said he didn't want to be an Ender anymore, not if he had to take orders like that again. He wanted to see our baby grow, not always fear that he would be taken from us. And he was."

Smoke moved up beside me. "Lana, what do you mean take orders like that?"

Lana's eyes flicked to Smoke. "That he was to kill the Enders from the Rim. He said it was wrong, but he didn't have a choice. He was fine, just fine in the healer's rooms. But you came back, didn't you?" Her glare found me and held me tightly. "You came back and finished the job you started, you hateful bitch." She launched herself at me and I again caught her, despite the lines of power racing up her arms. I didn't want her to fall, didn't want to hurt the child in her any more than I already had by taking its father away.

Catching her around the waist as she stumbled and spun, her back pressed to my front, and my hands ended up on her belly. Spirit roared forth within me and slid through us both. I saw her baby, saw his spirit and the beat of his heart. He would follow in his father's footsteps, be a warrior, if he survived his birth. The cord connecting him to his mother was wrapped three times around his neck.

"You're going to have a boy," I said, holding her lightly. She relaxed in my arms, placing her hands on my mine.

"How do you know—"

"The birth will be easy. You won't feel much pain, but the cord is around his neck. Three times. The midwife will know what to do."

I helped her stand on her own feet, the words flowing out my mouth. "He will be an Ender, like his father. A good man."

The images left me, and I put a hand to my head. Lana took my wounded hand, frowning at it as if looking for an answer. "You didn't mean to hurt him, did you?"

"No, I only wanted to get out alive," I said.

She nodded. "As do we all." With a flick of her wrist, she

dropped my hand and walked away, her friends following. But not before each of them stopped in front of me and spit at my feet.

Peta, I'd almost forgotten she was on my shoulder, grunted. "That little gesture means they wouldn't spit on you even if you were on fire."

"Nice."

Beside me, Smoke let out a long breath. "That could have been worse."

"The Enders, were they *all* healing that first night?" I asked and Smoke looked away.

"I am forbidden to say," she whispered.

"Forbidden? Or bound?" I asked as I scooped up the overturned laundry basket. There was ash on the clothes, but I wasn't about to stick my hands back into the river.

"Both."

"So I have to figure this out myself? That's what you're telling me?"

The tip of Peta's tail flicked along my neck, and I reached up to touch her, finding comfort in her presence. Smoke, though, said nothing, and I assumed that was my answer.

We headed back the way we'd come, climbing the steps into the higher parts of the cavern, the air drying my skin, hair and clothes in a matter of minutes.

"Perhaps I should take you to your friend, Cactus," Smoke said. "You can do work for him, help him clean his bachelor home."

I nodded. "Smoke, what about our ambassador here? Could he not stand for Ash in some way?"

She shook her head slowly. "The queen had all ambassadors sent home when things started to go poorly with the lava flows. She did not want to be responsible for them."

Damn, there would be no help from that quarter then.

Smoke walked with me across the high arched bridge to

the far side of the cavern where the singles lived. I wondered why they kept them apart from the families, and Peta must have picked up on my curiosity.

"The men when not bound to a wife can be out of control with their tempers and wild ways. No one wants that near their family," Peta said, filling me in as we walked.

"How old are they when they move here?" I asked, thinking of Brand and Smoke's son Stryker. He couldn't be that far from an age where he was considered an adult.

"Eighteen," Smoke said.

"And your son, how old is he?"

Her tone trembled. "He has a year left in our home."

There were no more words as we approached the singles section. It was remarkably quiet.

"They are all kept very busy. It helps with the male aggression to keep them tired."

"I saw him, in the throne room when we were brought in." I peered around, wondering which place belonged to Cactus.

Or maybe he lived with a woman. The thought was odd. Cactus had been a player from the beginning, chasing the pretty girls and stealing kisses whenever he could. I had a hard time seeing him settling down anytime soon.

Smoke stopped in front of one of the many doors. Made of a light green granite, the surface was cool even in the heat. I would have said it was beautiful, except unlike the other doors, it was . . .disgusting. Covered in patches of ash, and some sort of dark brown mud, it looked as though Cactus had never wiped it off. The rest of his home was no better, the place was like a human garbage dump, as if whoever lived there was collecting crap just for the sake of piling it in front of their house. I looked past it to the next door down the way, hoping I was wrong in my suspicion. "This is his home?"

She nodded and Peta let out a low hiss. "Disgusting man."
I couldn't disagree with her.

I took a step forward and stopped, imagining walking in on him and his latest conquest. Erring on the side of caution, I called out, "Cactus?"

There was a scuffle of feet and then he poked his head out of the doorway, saw me, and frowned. "Lark, what are you doing here?"

Confusion filtered through me and on its heels sharp irritation. "Well, I was brought here to be executed by your queen. So . . . yeah, I didn't have much choice in the matter, fool."

He shook his head, his dark red hair slicked back as if he'd come from bathing. With his green eyes, it was easy to see why the ladies flocked to him. Except for my disastrous foray into the Pit that had started this whole fiasco, I hadn't seen him since we'd been children. I realized I really didn't know if I could trust him. I didn't even know if he'd helped or deliberately made it harder for us—Ash and me—to survive our last visit. I took a step back, suddenly reconsidering my decision to ask him for help.

Smoke let out a soft snort. "You could at least show us some manners, boy."

His jaw tightened. "It's really not a good time."

I knew it. "Too many women in there? It's not like I'm going to be shocked, Cactus."

His mouth tightened farther and I wondered at how I'd possibly upset him. He'd bragged as a kid that he'd have all the ladies fawning over him one day. So now he had what he wanted, what was the issue?

Beside me Smoke snapped her fingers. "Cactus, this is ridiculous. Invite us in. You do not want to have this conversation outside."

He swiped a hand over his face, clearing away the

irritation, replacing it with a false smile that almost trembled. "Would you like to come in?"

I no longer did, but I had to find a way to get Ash out alive and that meant I needed all the help I could get. Even if Cactus wasn't the man I thought he should be.

Stepping through the doorway, I didn't know what to expect. Filthy, dirty clothes everywhere, food piled up and rotting. My imagination did not prepare me in the least.

I had to blink several times to really grasp what I was seeing. His house was an explosion of greenery and flowers, smells that took me back to the Rim. From the ceiling, plants and flowers curled down, covering every inch of exposed rock. The walls were blanketed in ivy and blackberry vines heavy with perfect black fruit. Under our feet the moss was so thick I could believe there was no stone beneath us. Down the wall, a trickle of water ran, feeding the plants and tiny flowers, the sound a perfect, soothing echo in the small space. Was this why he didn't want us to come in?

I closed my eyes and breathed in. "Cactus, this is amazing."

"You like it?"

I opened my eyes to see him watching me, his look carefully guarded. "Like it? It's just like home."

A slow breath escaped him. I glanced at Smoke to see her eyes wide. "How did you manage to get all this to grow?"

"Oh, I still carry a little of my connection to the earth," Cactus said softly, his hands brushing against a fern at his side. It leaned toward him and in that moment I knew something was terribly wrong. He shouldn't have been able to use so much of the earth's power. That was why his mother sent him to the Pit so many years ago; he had no power in the earth. That was the major drawback to being a half-breed. They were often weak not just in one of their bloodlines, but both. That Cactus had shown any strength at all was a miracle.

Yet if that rule held true, how could this be? How could he draw on both his bloodlines? Or maybe he was like me, an anomaly with that ability.

"Cactus." Just his name and his eyes lifted to mine. What I saw made my mouth dry. He was terrified. "Smoke, would you leave us please?" I never took my eyes from his.

"Are you sure?"

"Peta and Cactus can look out for me." I spit out the words fast, knowing the longer Smoke was there, the more fear built in Cactus. Smoke touched my arm and I forced myself to turn from Cactus to meet her eyes. I put a hand over hers. "Thank you."

Her eyes were tight around the edges. "Lark. You may not have an execution over your head but there are those who would still see you dead. An accident can happen all too easily as you have already seen."

"I will heed your words." I squeezed her hand and she stepped back, pausing in the doorway, her eyes flicking over the greenery.

"You are right to hide this, Cactus. The queen . . . she is strange about other powers in her home. But your secret will be safe with me, you are not the only one who hides." She placed a hand over her heart and then kissed her fingertips. A slight breeze lifted her hair and swirled from her hands, out and around the ferns. Another half-breed, like us. Without another word, Smoke stepped out of Cactus's house.

Peta leapt from my shoulders onto the mossy ground. "Dirt Girl, is your home like this?"

"Parts of it."

"I could handle being your familiar if this is what my paws get to be on." She lifted her feet up and down in exaggerated steps several times.

Smiling, I turned back to Cactus. He took three strides and wrapped an arm around my waist. "I've waited all my life for this, Lark."

He dropped his head and pressed his lips against mine.

Chapter 6

His hands slid up my waist to my back, tugging me closer. All my childhood feelings for him that I'd thought were gone and dead, blossomed under his touch. I could almost feel him laughing as he kissed me, his lips and tongue teasing my mouth. Making me want to laugh with him despite the fact that I was in the Pit, Ash's life hung in the balance, and someone tried to boil me.

That was Cactus, his love of life was infectious, but sometimes it got in the way.

I put my hands on his shoulders and turned my face. "Cactus, don't. Please."

"You aren't with Coal anymore. I heard that through the grapevine." He reached out and touched a hanging bunch of grapes to the right of us, a smile on his lips. I laughed softly.

"Stop. You're right I'm not with Coal . . ."

He raised an eyebrow but didn't let go of me with his other hand. "But?"

I didn't know what to say or how to explain Ash, because even I didn't really know what was going on there. "I'm just not . . .I have to focus on getting Ash and me out of here. And I need your help."

His eye green eyes lowered then slowly rose to mine. "And we can have this conversation after?"

I couldn't help the laugh with those puppy dog eyes he was laying on me. "Fine. We'll have this conversation after."

He let go of me and glanced to the floor. "What are you doing with the bad luck cat?"

Peta let out a low growl. "I'm her familiar, prick."

His eyebrows shot straight up. "Truly?"

"Yes. Listen. I need you to focus. Can you do that?" I asked, hoping I could get him to be serious for at least a few minutes.

"For you, Larkspur, princess of the Rim, of course."

"Princess?" Peta spit out the word with enough shock to make me blush.

""Bastard child," I said.

Cactus grunted. "The only bastards in the Rim were your siblings and Cassava."

Taking me by the hand he drew me deeper into the house. The greenery he'd been growing wasn't any thinner the farther back we went. If anything, the walls were thicker with the growth. "Cactus, how are you hiding this?"

He stopped in front of another door and slowly pushed it open. "I have to get out of here too, Lark. Whatever you're planning, I'm in. Because if I don't escape soon . . . Smoke is right. Fiametta is a hard ass and the fact I can do this much with the earth will either make her want to kill me or use me more than she already is."

I followed him into what I belatedly realized was his bedroom. "Cactus, I said we'd discuss our relationship later, but I didn't mean a few minutes later."

He held up his hands, finally letting go of me. "It's safer back here. Less chance of someone listening in."

Peta trotted forward, the white tip in her tail twitching several times as she sniffed the room. "He's right. The green stuff blocks the echo of voices the queen's spies could listen to through the rock."

Too much information at the same time made my head hurt. "Echo through the rock?"

Cactus flopped onto his bed, the woven vines and thick moss giving under his weight. He tucked his hands behind his head, his lean muscular body a rather inviting picture. He gave me a wink as if the fool knew what I was thinking. I fought the heat that rose in my cheeks. He spoke as though he hadn't noticed though. "Echo in the rock. The queen has Listeners who use the residual fire molecules within the rock to spy on her people. The plants muffle our voices."

I sank to sit on the bed beside him. Peta jumped into my lap and I put a hand on her, finding once more a comfort in her presence I hadn't expected. She looked to my face. "Dirt Girl, you can't save them all from their own queen. If you want to get your fellow Ender out, then that's what we need to focus on. What Brand asks of you could work in your favor."

Scratching one finger under her chin, I watched as her eyes closed and a low purr rumbled out of her. Her eyes popped open and she glared at me. "No amount of chin scratches will change what I suggest."

Cactus sat up. "If you need to get Ash out, then we need to play by the rules. Fiametta is a stickler for them. Which is why I hide this." He waved his hand as if to encompass the room. "She has stated that half breeds can only exist here if they don't touch their other half without her permission. Which isn't an issue for most since there are very few who can actually do anything." He ran a hand through his slicked back hair.

"But when did you find you could reach so much of the earth?" I found myself dropping my voice. Knowing Fiametta could be listening in was downright creepy.

"When I hit puberty. It was like something inside me opened and suddenly I could make things grow. And as you can imagine, a talent like that is valuable here."

"So Fiametta probably wouldn't banish you." I frowned, running the possibilities through my head. "But she'd force you to work for her, like a Planter?"

"Worse," Peta said softly. "She'd tell everyone he'd died and then keep him for herself, deep within her palace."

I stared down at Peta. "You know that for sure?"

She nodded. "You remember Loam? That was why he was in the Deep, to find weak Undines he could bring back with him for Fiametta. They draw the water up through the earth, bringing us the clean water we need. Same with the Sylphs, they funnel the fresh air and oxygen that the mountain and lava devour."

"Mother goddess," I breathed out, the enormity of what Peta and Cactus were telling me overshadowing the fact I had to find a way to get us out of the Pit. Fiametta was using slaves? The Undines used human slaves, but that was . . . different. Maybe it wasn't. I squeezed my eyes shut. Slavery was forbidden amongst all four elemental families. How in the seven hells was Fiametta getting away with this?

"They aren't slaves," Peta said. "They sign a contract stating they will be cared for if they do as they're asked. If they don't then they will be killed."

Cactus choked and his eyes widened. "That is just slavery with a contract."

Peta nodded. "Still, it is a loophole the rulers here have used for years. They all do it, just to different degrees."

"That's not true in the Rim," I said. "There is no slavery there."

Two sets of green eyes turned my way and I didn't like what I saw in them. Pity and disbelief.

My jaw tightened. "There is no slavery in the Rim, but I'm not going to argue about that right now. We have far more pressing matters."

The urgency of my task suddenly seemed overwhelming. I had to get us out of the Pit before anything could be done about the slavery Fiametta was enforcing.

All four of us had to be free of the Pit and the inherent dangers within it.

"Peta," I scooped her up so I could lift her to my eye level. "Are you really with me? Can I trust you with my life?"

Her cat lips dipped in a perfect frown. "The mother goddess assigned me to you herself. It is my job to help you stay alive."

"That's not what I'm asking." I stared into those green eyes as the idea that had formed within my mind grew. Peta knew the Pit, probably better than Cactus, and she was all but ignored because of her status. Which made her the perfect spy. But so much of my plan depended on being able to trust my familiar. "Peta, are you with me?"

She blinked several times before she answered. "You're going to be the death of all nine of my lives, aren't you?"

"I hope not."

She snorted and her ears twitched. "I am with you, Dirt Girl. What are you going to ask of me?"

"Can you get into the Ender Barracks? There is an Ender with a scar on the top of his right hand. I need to know his name."

She squirmed out of my hands. "What does the scar look like?"

I squatted beside her, and turned my hand palm down. The scars on my hand from Peta grabbing me had faded to silvery lines. While they were not ridged like the ones the Ender sported, but they were similar enough. "Like my scars only thicker, like a bigger cat maybe clawed him."

Peta looked at me, her eyes narrowed to mere slits making it impossible to read her. "He should be easy to find. Why do you want him?"

"He's a traitor to the queen. If we give him to her, I think we should be able to bargain for Ash's life," I said. Cactus gave a low grunt.

"You do not know her very well then."

I looked at Peta. "And what do you think, cat? You think the queen will not bargain?" It wasn't my only option, but I needed a way to buy Ash time. Time I needed to find a permanent way out.

"Cactus is right. She won't bargain." Peta shook her head, her ears twitching. "But it might buy us time if you offer her a traitor on a platter. She likes nothing more than to wield the Lava Whip herself on those she deems deserving of punishment."

I didn't want to ask what the Lava Whip was. I could easily guess. A shiver ran down my spine. "Time is better than nothing. See if you can find the Ender I described to you. But be careful."

Peta bobbed her head and ran down the hallway, her tiny footsteps eaten by the moss. I bit my lower lip and closed my eyes. "Cactus, we may all end up in the fire if this goes wrong."

He stood, moving to my side and draping an arm across my shoulders. "We all end up in the fire at some point, Lark. But if anyone can get us there sooner, it's you." At my incredulous expression, Cactus fell back onto the mossy mattress. "I'm kidding, Lark."

I plopped onto the springy edge. He sat down beside me and brushed a hand over my hair, so gently I barely felt his touch; it was more a sense of knowing him, and his intentions. "You've always been special, Lark. When I heard about Cassava's trickery . . . and how you faced her down with nothing but a spear; that you saved your entire family, I wasn't surprised. After that some of my memories came back." The last was said in a near whisper.

I swallowed hard. "You remember the day in the meadow?"

The day my mother and brother were killed.

He nodded, dropping his head to press it against mine. "I think maybe Cassava blocked some of my abilities too, keeping me weak. The longer I was away from her, the longer I was here in the Pit, the stronger I got."

A shudder danced along my spine and I let myself relax against him. "I'm sorry she hurt you too."

His hand rubbed along my back. "Meh. I'm tough for a fool."

Laughing, I turned to face him, but the laughter died quickly. "Smoke said something that might save Ash faster than finding a traitor. Something that Lana confirmed whether she meant to or not."

Cactus leaned back on his elbows, his eyes thoughtful. "If anyone has an inkling of a rumor, it'll be Smoke. People don't see her. They treat her poorly because she's a half breed." He jerked upright. "Wait, you saw Lana?"

"She was at the water. It was not a good scene."

I leaned back beside him and we lay down at the same time, staring up at the ceiling and the wisteria that hung like pale purple bunches of grapes, the scent of the flowers flowing around us. "Smoke said something about the

Enders who were killed. That maybe it wasn't the injuries we—I—inflicted but something else. And Lana confirmed it. She said she saw her husband that night. He was fine and healing, and the next morning he was dead. His wounds opened and left to die."

Turning my head to the side I stared at his profile, but he didn't turn to me. He kept looking at the ceiling. "The question is, who would want to hurt them?"

That was the question I was asking myself. "I don't know. Does Fiametta have anyone vying for her throne?" I was thinking of my trip to the Deep and the battle for the crown that had nearly taken my, Belladonna's, and Ash's lives. I was really hoping that wasn't the case again. Two powerful battling fire elementals was not something I wanted to get in the middle of.

"No. Everyone is terrified of her. She's a hard ass, in the truest sense of the words, Lark. There is no room for softness in her. If you're useful, you're good in her eyes. If you aren't, she has no room for you." He draped an arm over his forehead.

"And what is your use for her?" I reached up and touched his fingers. I wanted him to look at me. His voice wasn't giving me any indication as to how he was feeling.

Cactus learned to hide as well as I had as a child in the forest. "Cactus, what are you afraid of? Because if it was just a matter of the queen, you'd leave."

He was silent for a good minute before he answered, his voice carefully neutral.

"Because of my connection to the earth, I can do more damage than most Salamanders. Within the fire are particles of rock and granite so my blows are a double hit if I'm defending our people against the firewyrms who lurk below us." He finally turned to me. His green eyes held more than a measure of pain. "I'm not an Ender, Lark. Not like you. I'm just a tool used at her discretion. I'm the threat behind her words and that is why escaping her is going to be so hard."

I reached out and smoothed the lines between his brows. There were no words I could say, nothing to make it better. But my heart ached at the thought of losing not only Ash, but Cactus too. No, I couldn't let that happen.

I wished I knew exactly how I was going to stop both men from being lost to Fiametta.

Chapter 7

Laying on Cactus's bed, I closed my eyes and breathed in the green scents, letting them soothe my mind and body, the strength of them flowing through my bruised and battered arm and hand. Somewhere in that spot between wakefulness and sleep, I floated, recharging all I was. Cactus curled his body around me and I held onto him like I'd done more than once as a child. We had to wait on Peta anyway, so the guilt I felt at lying quietly and resting while Ash lay in a dungeon, eased.

As children, Cactus and I had clung to each other in the dark of the night as we shared stories of monsters creeping out of the Deep or the Pit, of winged beasts flying from the Eyrie to steal bad Terralings away. Now, those stories seemed more possible than ever and it was in that moment the image flickered through my mind of the massive doors leading to the throne room and the dragon carved into it. No wings, a sinuous body, and all the gemstones around it, the malice just the image gave off.

Firewyrms were the stuff of legend, even in the Rim, yet even as I thought of the creature, I dismissed it. There was no way firewyrms were here. Not a chance. Cactus had to be joking as he so often had when we were children.

The soft give of the bed under weight brought me around and I slowly opened my eyes. Peta's green eyes stared into mine. "The Ender you're looking for is nowhere to be found, Dirt Girl." She pushed herself under my jaw, curling into the space between my chest and chin, her head resting in the crook of my neck. "Perhaps he is one of the Enders you killed."

I reached up and touched her back, the calming energy on either side of me allowing me to think clearly. "No, he was part of the group that brought me and Ash in. I wouldn't have seen his memories otherwise, so he has to be here somewhere."

What would I do if I couldn't find the traitor to hand to Fiametta to in turn buy Ash time? The only other person I could ask was Brand, but despite the fact he was Ash's friend, I wasn't sure how much he could do bound to Fiametta. Only one way to find out, and that would be to ask him who was with the posse to get us from the Rim.

Holding Peta to me, I sat up and then stood. "Cactus, I have to go."

"I'm coming with you." He scrubbed a hand through his hair making it stick up in a riotous mess. "I couldn't help you much the last time you were here. The queen was watching me closely."

"Why?" Peta asked before I could spit it out.

He gave us a lopsided grin. "I turned down her invitation to her bedroom."

Peta made a sound that was a mix between a hiss and a snort that I thought might have been a gasp. Spluttering, she managed to spit out, "How are you still alive?"

Cactus shrugged, but his lips twitched. "I told her my heart was broken by someone from the Rim, and I'd sworn celibacy to the mother goddess."

I lowered Peta to the floor where she glared at Cactus, her thoughts all but written on her face. She didn't believe him.

My turn. "And she believed you?"

"I told her the princess I loved still held my heart and I could never be unfaithful to her, even if I could never be with her." Cactus's tone was light and teasing but in the depths of his eyes I saw the yearning. The truth behind his words. I was the one he wanted. I was the princess sworn to another.

I looked away. "Peta, why would Fiametta buy that?"

"I'm surprised she did," Peta said. "But that doesn't mean it can't happen. The queen keeps things close to her chest and lets no one in. Not even her children."

I walked out of the room and down the hall. "You can come, Cactus. But if for one instant Fiametta starts to pay attention to you—"

"I'll back out. Don't worry so much, Lark. This will be slick as slug spit." He jogged to catch up to me, swatting me lightly on the ass with an open palm. I arched an eyebrow at him.

"Cactus." Just his name, a simple warning. Peta was less subtle.

"Keep your hands to yourself, prick."

The three of us stepped out of Cactus's place and into the open cavern and just for a moment, disorientation flowed over me. Going from the green, cool, and flowering place that Cactus had created to the stark rock of the inner mountain I had to take a few breaths and get my bearings. The heat picked up with each step we took, like being inside a tiny box, we couldn't escape the closed in air and for just a moment panic reared its head.

I wanted to run, to get to Brand as quick as possible and ask him who was with us when we'd Traveled; just to get this over with. But if Cactus was right and the queen had her spies watching everyone, listening to everything, I had to be careful.

Walking swiftly, I headed back to the bridge. I stepped onto the arched structure and bolted across. The heat from the lava flowed through the rock that made up the bridge despite how thick each piece of stone was.

Peta trotted across, her tail flicking in the air and Cactus sauntered, smiling at me the whole way. I shook my head and spun, stepping right into the chest of a well-endowed woman. Bouncing off her, I took a couple steps back. "I'm sorry."

She was almost as tall as my six feet, which was unusual. Her hair was so dark a red, it was almost a purple tone, and her eyes were a pale gray. Other than her large chest, it was difficult to tell she was a woman. Her shoulders were incredibly broad and her hips narrow but between hips and shoulders she had a monstrous gut.

She arched an eyebrow at me. "Terraling. What are you doing wandering around?"

Peta strode between us, shifting into her full leopard form, her black spotted thick white coat rippling. "I'm watching over her, Fay. Leave the Dirt Girl to me."

Fay let out a low laugh. "Oh, then she'll be dead within the week. Well done, bad luck cat." She patted Peta's head and strolled away, still laughing. I took a step forward and touched Peta's head.

"Don't listen to them," I said, knowing what it was to be the one your people looked down on.

Peta let out a low growl. "We are not friends, Dirt Girl. Not by a long shot. I do this because I must." She shrunk back to her housecat form and stiff legged, stalked away from me.

Cactus was at my side a second later. "She's . . .touchy. In all the four families, Peta has lost the most charges. They always die on her, and the mother goddess doesn't seem inclined to stop handing her off to people."

"Lovely. And now everyone will think I'm next on the list."

"Why do you think Peta hasn't told anyone she's your familiar unless she has to?" Cactus arched an eyebrow at me and I realized he had a point. As long as Peta kept quiet, no one would make the connection between us and when I died, it would be one less death on her.

Damn, that was a tough row to hoe.

"I hate to disappoint her, but I don't plan on dying anytime soon," I muttered as I walked after my familiar. My familiar. That had a nice ring to it, even if Peta hated me. Maybe I could get a new familiar once this was all over. One that could tolerate me and would be nice.

Peta waited quietly outside Smoke and Brand's house. She sat and stared past me, her green eyes unblinking, and she said nothing. Fine by me.

I put a hand to the edge of the door and peered in. "Smoke?"

Not Smoke but their youngest boy, Tinder answered me. "Hi, Terraling. My mom isn't here right now." He grinned up me, two front teeth missing on the top of his jaw. I smiled back.

"Actually, I was wondering if you knew where your dad was?"

He bobbed his head several times and for just a moment I saw Cactus as he'd been as a child. Always eager to be a part of whatever was going on. "Yup. He's down by the edge of the Pit. But I think that's too hot for you. You'll burn up."

I forced myself to smile, because he was right. I had no protection from the heat and flames. "Thanks, I'll be careful."

"I could take you there. I was just swimming there with my brothers." He slapped a hand over his mouth and I remembered Smoke told him specifically not to swim at the Pit. I shook my head. "It's okay. I've got Cactus here to take me."

Cactus gave the boy a wink. "Besides, you wouldn't want your dad seeing you find your way to the Pit on your own when you aren't supposed to even know where it is, right?"

Tinder nodded, his eyes solemn. "You're right." He spun and ran back into the house before I could say goodbye.

Beside me, Cactus chuckled. "They all find their way to the Pit before they're supposed to."

I glanced at Peta. "You coming?"

She flicked an ear at me, stretched and sauntered out in front of us. I lifted an eyebrow at Cactus. "You still want to come with me? I'm sure Peta can take me there with no problem."

His green eyes sparkled. "You're going to need me, Lark. I just know it. So yes, I'm coming with you."

I wasn't arguing with him. He had gained strength in his abilities in our years apart and now was the queen's threat against whatever they were afraid of. Not a bad guy to have on my team while I attempted the impossible. We walked the length of the cavern, and at the far end, a cut in the rock opened. Stairs led downward, and the same light reflecting in tunnels that I'd seen in Cactus's home and the main cavern were used to illuminate the darkness.

"How far down?" I put my foot on the first step, the rock warm under my bare feet.

"Long," Peta said. "It will take at least half an hour to get to the bottom."

Damn, that was a long ways down. But if I hurried, I was sure I could cut the time in half. Jogging down the stairs, I easily kept pace with Peta who was running ahead, the white tip of her tail twitching side to side as she leapt down each stair.

"Lark, slow down." Cactus caught up to me and touched my arm. I glanced at him.

"What are you talking about?"

"You're running as if you're in a hurry," he said, his own pace slowing, his hand dragging at me.

Frowning, I didn't slow. "We *are* in a hurry. Ash's life is on the line and I was just lying on my back in your room as if there was nothing in the world to—"

"Easy, easy. I know. But you had to heal and that was as good a place as any to let your body pull together while we waited for Peta. The thing is . . . if you look like you're in a hurry, people are going to notice you more. You don't want that, Lark. You don't want to be noticed here." He stared straight ahead, his thumbs hooked into his belt as he walked slowly.

Painstakingly slow. Peta turned her head and let out a sneeze. "He's right."

Damn it, I just wanted to get to Brand before the day was over. That was the other part of being in the Pit that weighed on me. How many hours had gone by? How would I know when I had only a day left? The lack of sun was fouling my ability to gauge time.

And I said as much to Cactus, but Peta answered.

"Everyone goes to sleep when night falls; that is how you know the day is over. And when you wake, the new day has started." She slowed and I bent to pick her up, only touching her when she gave me a bob of her head.

Placing her on my shoulder, I kept walking, forcing my feet to go slow even as they itched to run. "That seems . . . odd."

"It's how the Pit has been run for as long as I can remember." Peta wrapped her tail around my neck as she perched on my left shoulder like some sort of oversized bird that was currently purring. I chose not to point out she was obviously enjoying my company; the connection between us was growing in leaps and bounds.

In the back of my head I sensed her emotions and general thoughts. Nothing specific, but more of an overview of where she was in her feelings and mindset. Already I could tell she was secretly pleased I had listened to her, and while she was far from happy that I was her new charge, she didn't really hate me.

I forced my thoughts back to the whole sleeping business. "So what makes everyone fall asleep? Or is there like a gong that sounds and everyone just goes to bed?"

Cactus shook his head. "No gong, a bell. First the bell chimes, then you get a warning that sleep is coming from a tingling in the spine that spreads through your body. Enough time to get to a bed and lie down."

"And if you don't?"

He answered, "You fall asleep wherever you are. Sometimes people get caught in the tunnels and sleep the night on the hard stone."

The bottom of the stairs flattened out into a large chunk of quartz smoothed and polished to a high sheen under our feet. The rock protruded out into open space all the way around the edge of the cavern we were in. A platform if I ever saw one. Cactus pointed past me toward the flickering sparks of fire that rose up from below. "This is the Pit. You sure you want to go in?"

"No choice," I said. And there wasn't, not if I wanted to save Ash.

Chapter 8

The platform was warm under my feet as I stepped onto it, my toes curling against the stone. Heat waves rolled up in rippling shadows that filled the air. I couldn't see the lava, but I heard it burping and plopping as it boiled far below. Swallowing hard, I forced myself to step farther onto the platform. The smooth rock ran a good twenty feet deep all the way around the edge of the Pit and it reminded me all too strongly of the Deep and their mini coliseum. Was this a platform to watch people fight to the death within the lava? Mother goddess I hoped not.

At various and seemingly random points along the edge of the platform, stairs curled downward to the main floor where a few Salamanders walked. One was swimming in the lava. My brain still struggled to comprehend how that was possible.

I took another step and a tiny set of claws dug into my right shoulder.

"Lark, do not walk to the edge. Go to your belly. If you get a waft of fumes, you could pass out and fall in," Peta said.

Worm shit, I hadn't thought about that. I nodded and dropped to my knees, slid down to my belly, and then scooted forward. Cactus did the same, inching up beside me. I peered over the edge of the rock, and Peta scooted across my spine to sit on the back of my shoulders. But that was a distant sensory to what I saw.

Lava indeed. The Pit was one monstrous magma pool that stretched several hundred feet across with tendrils reaching out; rivers that spread through the mountain. Orange and reds, yellows and golds so intense that my eyes hurt looking at the pool. Waves of heat wafted off the surface, curling into the air, bringing the smell of burnt things and sulfur.

"Hypnotizing." I scooted a little farther forward to get a better look and Peta's claws tipped into me again.

"No swimming," she said.

I shook my head, but Cactus still grabbed my hand, his fingers lacing tightly with mine.

"Just in case." He winked at me, a grin tugging at his lips.

Leaning over the edge, I gripped his hand. Something was pulling me, urging me to get closer. The soft whisper of words barely spoken, teased my ears. Someone was close below us and something about the voices made me think it would be worth listening in on.

I looked at Cactus and pointed at my feet. I barely breathed the words, "Hold my ankles."

"Lark don't—"

But I didn't give him a choice. I wriggled over the edge, forcing him to grab me.

He shimmied back and grabbed my ankles even as he grumbled, helping me slide over the edge. Peta said nothing, but clung to my back, digging her claws into my leather vest like a burr tangled in my hair.

Even those few inches closer to the lava, the increased heat made sweat pop out over my body in a vain attempt to cool my temperature. The heat dried the sweat as fast as it slid down my sides.

Gripping the granite cliff, I dug my fingers into the rock, imagining it softening enough to get a better hold. The rock gave under my hands and I stared at the granite, swallowing my surprise. I quickly shaped the rock into perfect handholds. Peta grunted, her voice in my ear, a bare whisper. "We need to discuss this later. You shouldn't be able to mold rock like that."

As interesting as that little tidbit was, I had more pressing things on my mind.

Using my handholds and trusting Cactus, I slid a few more inches until I could see underneath the platform toward the whispering I was sure I heard.

The shadowed overhang made it hard to make out what was going on.

A tiny flash of movement, the soft muttering of words I felt I should understand; a language I'd heard maybe when I was a child. Narrowing my eyes, I shifted another inch and then went still. My hair swept out around my head, dangling a good foot lower. Whoever was down there was bound to see it. I should have tied it up but it was too late now.

Pale white scales flickered up at me, and two pairs of eyes the color of amethyst blinked several times. The firewyrms were small, maybe the length of my legs at most and curled around each other. They looked like wingless, sinewy dragons. Their mouths had row upon row of needle sharp teeth I had no doubt would rip through armor, rock, and maybe even hardened steel.

The one in front had a scar down its left side, the scales missing in a long, jagged line. Scar stepped closer to me and let out a long, low hiss that ended in a gurgle.

"Cactus," I said, keeping my voice as even and smooth as possible. "Tell me about firewyrms."

"Oh shit, those bastards are causing problems. Nesting where they shouldn't and then attacking when people—wait, why would you ask me that now?" His hands tightened on my ankles and he started to pull me up but I grabbed onto the rock. Scar's eyes, they held a world of hurt and fear. A child lost.

I couldn't help myself.

Jerking my feet out of Cactus's hands, I swung my legs over and into the shallow notched space. Peta let out a squawk and her tiny body tightened as we landed in a crouch. The firewyrms scuttled backward, mouths open as they threatened, but no fire erupted, no flames came our way.

Peta bit my ear, her sharp teeth piercing the cartilage. "You idiot, I said I didn't want you to die, and you drop into a wyrm nest? What's wrong with you?"

Heart pounding, I didn't move, didn't even stand. "Hey, you two, I heard you talking." On my shoulder, Peta went still. "You shouldn't be able to understand them, Dirt Girl."

I held a hand out to them. "Who hurt you?"

Scar looked over his shoulder, quickly to his sibling then stretched his neck forward. He squinted one eye as a long forked tongue flicked toward me. His scales were more than white, they were opalescent with rainbow colors dancing on them, as they caught a bit of light. With each step he took toward me, his clawed feet clacked on the stone.

His headgear was six long antelope-like antlers that arched back over his neck away from his long muzzle. The same pale white horns spiked from his elbows and the bend in his hind legs. With a whip-like tail that was barbed at the end, I had no doubt he could lash out for a distance. Topping it off were his claws. Five on each foot, and at least twelve inches long, they seemed oversized for his body.

Yet fear still didn't touch me.

My heart pounded and the blood roared in my ears, like an oncoming storm that would be amazing. Or terrifying. Or both.

That long tongue flicked over my fingers and then he scuttled backward, his lips curling upward. Peta clung to me, breathing so hard she panted in my ear. "Dirt Girl, we need to go. He will fry us both."

I put a hand on her in an attempt to ease her trembling. "Scar, what happened to you?"

He rolled his head so he looked at me upside down. "Vy do you care?"

His voice was pitched low enough that I knew now why I'd struggled to understand. He had an accent.

"I don't like any of the mother goddess's creatures to suffer," I said, holding my hand out to him again. A show of trust, and faith that he wouldn't fry us, as Peta said.

Peta meowed and buried her head against my neck, her whole body shaking. Scar slid forward and pressed his nose against the palm of my hand.

A quiet sigh slipped out of him. "You smell nice."

"Thank you."

His eyes flicked to his sibling and then back to me. "Vy are you being nice to us?"

I stayed crouched so I was at eye level with him. "I'm hoping you can tell me about your people."

His head wove back and forth several times. "My people

are dying out. The fire queen hunts and kills us. Ve don't mean to attack, but ve can't help it. The pink light fills our minds and ve must obey."

His words couldn't have shocked me more. "Pink light?" As in the light I saw when elementals were controlled by Spirit. Was that what was happening?

Behind me was a thump of feet hitting the ground and Scar scuttled backward, hissing and snarling. "Hunter!"

I glanced over my shoulder, thinking I would see Cactus. But it was someone I didn't recognize. An Ender in black leathers and gloves was all I registered before he grabbed me and jerked me behind him. "Get back, idiot, you don't know what they are capable of."

I hit the ground, stumbling under the force of his throw, sliding to the edge unable to stop my momentum. I scrabbled at the rock, crying out as my body slipped into open space. Peta screeched, as the world turned upside down as I rolled in the air.

A flash of white scales and the world righted itself, or at least, stopped moving. I hung upside down and Peta clung to the front of my vest, her tail bristled out like a cotton puff.

"Peta, who grabbed us?"

"Your new friend," she whispered.

I managed to lean up and look past her. Scar clung to the cliff face, holding onto my leg with his long tail, the barb hooking over his own flesh to lock around my limb. His claws were buried into the stone and he slowly began to climb sideways.

Above us in the tiny cave came shouting and the sound of flesh being hit. "Hurry, Scar. Get me back up there."

He shook his head. "We can't save her. The Hunter will take her."

The mother goddess's words suddenly made sense. Lives to save . . . she didn't send me to save Ash.

She sent me to save the firewyrms.

"Scar, get me up there. Now!" Anger coursed through my veins; an anger born of understanding. To be treated as though you were worthless and should be wiped out . . . that I knew too well. I reached to the earth as Scar climbed swiftly up the rock, the power humming under my skin, filling me with its strength. A flick of his tail and I launched into the air and over the edge.

The other firewyrm lay unmoving, the Ender standing over her. He had one foot on her tail and his club dripped with blood.

"Get away from her." I whipped my hand out, calling the earth upward and throwing the Ender backward. He slammed into the far wall, his head snapping hard against the rock. Eyes rolled back, he slid to the ground in a slump.

I ran forward and dropped to my knees in front of the firewyrm. "Scar, does she have a name?"

"No, ve don't have names. Ve just are. You are the first to name one of us in a long time." His head pushed under my arm as I laid my hands on the white, still scales. No breath and her heartbeat was gone.

Peta let out a sigh. "Spirit can heal, Dirt Girl. I don't know how, but I know it can. If it isn't too late."

I didn't hesitate; if I were to lose a piece of my soul for saving another, then so be it.

Grappling with the other side of my bloodline, I brought Spirit forward. Like an unruly horse, it bucked and pulled from me, making me sweat as I tried to direct it. Why now? Before when I'd called on it, there had been no fight. But I'd not tried to heal anyone before, so maybe that was it.

I tried to be gentle as I pushed Spirit into the firewyrm,

directing it to flow through her muscles, into her heart, across her bones. Sweat dripping from my face, I gritted my teeth as I tried to bring her back.

Peta licked my cheek. "You can't save her, Dirt Girl. She's gone too long. That is why Spirit fights you, I believe. I think she was already beyond your reach."

I let go of Spirit and hung my head, tears dripping along with the sweat. "Then what is the point of being able to have Spirit if I can do nothing with it?"

Scar stuck his head onto my lap. "You tried. That is more than any others have done."

Wrapping my arm around his neck, I hugged him tightly to me before letting him go. "You'd better get out of here, the Ender will wake soon. Take your sister with you." I stood and Scar scuttled forward, scooping his sister onto his back.

"Be careful," he said, then disappeared over the side of the ledge once more. I followed, watching him slither down the vertical wall as if it were nothing to him. Glancing up, I realized that Cactus had been suspiciously absent.

"Cactus?"

Nothing.

I reached up and grabbed the handholds I'd made on my way down and pulled myself up. Peta leapt from my shoulders onto the top of the ledge.

"He's here, but . . . you aren't going to like this," she said. The tone in her voice made me scramble faster. I swung my legs up and over, scooting forward on my belly for a few feet before pushing to my knees.

Cactus was flat on his back, a large goose egg budding over his left eye. I ran one finger over it and brought Spirit forward again. It didn't fight me as I wove its strength through Cactus's body. I didn't really know what I was doing, letting Spirit do as it would.

The bump shrank until there was nothing, not even a

bruise on his skin. He blinked and sat up. "What the hell just happened? I was calling to you and then something slammed into my head and nothing until right now."

I gave him a weak grin. "What do you get when you find a firewyrm, fight an Ender, and fall off a cliff?"

"Shit." He stood and pulled me to my feet. "Where is the Ender?"

"Still in the cave down there."

"Tell me you didn't kill him," Cactus said, reaching for me. I frowned at him.

"I'm not an idiot. I just knocked him out."

Peta gave a full body shiver. "We must hide the fact that you attacked him, Dirt Girl. With Cactus's injury gone, we will all say we have no idea what that Ender is talking about when he accuses you. Do you understand?"

I nodded, but I wasn't sure it would work. Especially not when we turned to see we were not alone.

Fiametta stood behind us, her eyebrows arched high over her brilliant blue eyes, and her black leathers glistening in the flickering light around us. She seemed backlit by a pale pink light. My heart clenched. Was someone manipulating her even now?

But who?

"What does the Terraling not understand, Peta?"

Chapter 9

I dropped to one knee and pressed my hands into the rock, feeling the essence of the earth under my skin as Spirit still rode high through my veins. I could feel the beating heart of everyone within fifty feet, including the queen and the Ender below us.

Brand stared at me from a few steps behind the queen. "Terraling, you are supposed to be helping my wife."

Letting out a slow breath I nodded and stood, the instinct to connect to the earth something I'd not expected. "She sent me with Cactus, since I fell into the river helping her with the laundry."

Cactus tugged at my arm; I knew what he wanted. We hadn't addressed Fiametta yet. Faux pas number one.

"Your Majesty," I said.

"Terraling, I see you are getting the grand tour while your friend awaits his punishment. How lovely for you." Fiametta's voice cracked like a whip through the air and the men flinched. Peta clung to my shoulders, shaking once more. Behind the queen stood her black panther, Jag. His eyes were full of sorrow as he looked at me and then away. But he said nothing. No doubt the queen would just ignore him anyway. I watched as he turned and walked away, leaving his charge on her own.

So it was as Peta had said. The queen didn't use her familiar at all.

A scramble of rocks behind us stopped all conversation as the Ender who'd attacked me and Cactus pulled himself over the ledge.

The queen went to him. From where I stood, her movements softened as she held a hand to him. He kissed her offered hand, his lips lingering on her skin and I saw a quick flash of his tongue as it darted out.

Worm shit and green sticks, of course it would be her lover.

The epiphany hit me like a dozen redwoods crashing to the forest floor. If he was her lover, he was also the traitor. Son of a bitch, he couldn't have made it easier on us. If in fact, he was one and the same.

Eyes that were dark as night locked with mine as the Ender looked past his queen. "I don't believe we've been introduced, you wyrm lover." There it was, that same voice I'd heard in the memories.

Peta whispered in my ear. "He will not go down easy. Be wary."

Fiametta turned so she faced me. "Wyrm lover? Coal, what is going on?"

Coal. Of course, his name would be the same as *my*

ex-lover. Seemed fitting since I was about to ruin his life too. He stepped around her, a sly smile on his lips as he pointed a finger at me.

"She attacked me when I was trying to kill a pair of hatchlings."

I laughed, feeling the weight of the moment laying on me. If I didn't play this right, we would all be dead. I was not a consummate actress, but I had to try. "Please, why would I attack you? And what is this about a hatchling?"

He frowned and pointed to the back of his head. "I have a wound. And so does the prick. He tried to stop me and I clubbed him. Proof of my words."

The furrowed brows on Fiametta's face would have made me stop talking, but Coal kept on. She strode to Cactus who held very still, murmuring only a simple, "My queen."

Her hands roved his face and head, looking for an injury. "I see nothing here, Coal."

"Impossible. I heard his skull crack," he said and then seemed to swallow his words as Fiametta turned toward him.

Fiametta's eyes held flames. "You would attack my best defender, Ender? He is the first who stands between me and the firewyrms. That you would even admit this tells me how little you care for our safety. "

"Spitfire—"

I flinched as he used an obvious pet name for her. Her face paled and two bright red spots appeared high on her cheekbones. Coal swallowed whatever else he was going to say. Which was maybe his best decision of the day.

She raised her left hand and held it palm out toward him. "You are hereby stripped of your ranks, and all *privileges*. I see no wounds on Cactus, but he is a favored Salamander in our eyes and that you would even attack him leaves me questioning your loyalty."

Confidence soaring, I had to fight the smile that wanted to creep over my lips. This really was too easy. "He has a scar on his hand, does he not? Hidden under his glove."

Coal's whole body jerked as if I'd jammed my knee into his family jewels. Fiametta looked from him to me. "Ender, do you know this Terraling?"

"No, my queen." Interesting that his story was suddenly changing. Anything to keep on the queen's good side.

"Oh, sure you do," I said, feeling the weight of the situation as if a boulder lay across my shoulders and not a ten-pound house cat.

"I've never met her, my queen." He was sweating, and I didn't think it was heat. I glanced from him to Fiametta only to find her blue eyes staring at me.

I forced a smile to my lips as my mind raced. Think like Belladonna, that was all I could think. "Do you trust your Ender? Trust that he wouldn't lie to you? Oh, what am I saying, he did lie to you just now. Right to your face."

Her blue eyes narrowed to mere slits. "Terraling, you walk a fine line. Do remember that while you are here, you must abide by my rules until you leave. Or you will find yourself next to your friend making a last, short walk into the Pit together."

Damn, a fine line indeed. I lifted both hands, palms up and shrugged. "If you wish to bed a viper and think his bite is not venomous, then be my guest. I will say no more, per your wishes." Turning, I beckoned to Cactus whose face was slack as if I'd punched him in the mouth. "Cactus, you said you would show me the Pit as close as I could get?"

"Stop." Fiametta said, her voice icy cold, but power rumbled under it and the lava below us picked up in noise, as though fountains spurted with the wicked fire. There was no emotion in Fiametta's voice. I had her attention now. I turned expecting her command to be for me. It wasn't.

The Ender—her lover and traitor—was attempting to sprint away. Cactus stepped beside me, lifted his hand and the doorway that the Ender would have run through crumbled, most effectively stopping him.

He spun and lifted his club, pointing it at Fiametta. The fear on him was so thick it seemed to fill the air.

"You bitch, you have ruined this family!"

I was the closest one to him and I acted without truly considering what I was doing.

Pulling Peta from my shoulder I pushed her behind me as I sprinted forward, putting myself between the Ender and Fiametta—of course, I had no weapon.

The Ender laughed. "You think to protect her? She doesn't deserve your protection."

I settled into a fight stance. "Leave that to me to decide."

"Lark, here, you could need this." Brand called out as the sound of metal and wood scraped along the smooth granite. Rolling to a stop at my feet was my spear, the curved blade, and wooden handle once held by my mother. I scooped it up, and spun it toward the Ender as he raced toward me with his club. The blade caught on the dark stone as we twisted our weapons against one another. My muscles strained and my shoulder protested but I held him back, if only just barely.

"Coal, stop this," Fiametta said and for just a second I wanted to glance around for the dark hair and green eyes of my previous lover. But of course, this Coal was the Salamander in front of me. And I had no doubt he would kill me if I let my guard down for an instant.

"The last Coal I faced lost his hand," I said as I thrust my spear toward his belly, turning the move into a downward slash and catching his knee. The tip of my blade cut through his leathers and the side of his knee. He went down but swept his club in front of him keeping me away. His black eyes glittered with hate, and I read the understanding in them that he was going to die.

I took a step back, spinning my spear loosely in front of my body.

Fiametta stepped forward so we stood side by side, but her eyes were all for her lover. "You would kill me?"

He never lowered his eyes and I waited for the moment he would strike. "A thousand times over."

"Why?"

Coal shook his head. "I will say no more."

Fiametta tipped her head and I thought for a brief moment I saw a quiver of sorrow flicker over her face. "Coal, drop your weapons."

He shook his head as he slowly stood, hobbling on one leg. "No. Kill me and be done with it."

Fiametta spared me a look. "Can you take him without killing him?"

Here was a chance I would not have again to gain her good graces. "If that is what you wish."

"Do it."

I stepped in front of her again and slowly shifted my spear so I held the shaft near the blade and the blunt end was aimed at Coal.

"I will force you to kill me."

I had no doubt he would do just that. "Fiametta, will you allow me to question him?"

She snorted softly. "You think you can make him speak without torture?"

"I know more than he realizes," I said, the balls of my feet aching with the need to move. I reached for the part of me that was anything but Terraling. Spirit flowed through me and I focused on Coal. On loosening his tongue and making him spill his secrets. Coal eyed me up as he spoke.

"We never met, you never even looked my way when we picked you and your friend out of the Rim." His eyes bugged as he realized he spoke freely, doing exactly what he said he wouldn't.

"The first night you bedded the queen, you were searching for something in her room. What is it?" I asked.

Behind me Fiametta sucked in a sharp breath and Coal's eyes looked over my shoulder. Like the sound of a tornado being unleashed, the oxygen around me was sucked away in a gulping whoosh. A furred body hit me, slamming me to the ground. Peta in her full leopard form crouched over me as the wave of pure lava rolled through the air, and wrapped around Coal. The liquid fire shimmered and shifted in the air, a living coil of death rippling from the queen's outstretched hands.

Shifting my gaze back to Coal, I stared in horror as the lava wrapped around his middle. His head rolled back as a scream ripped from his mouth—a scream that turned into a gurgle—his body was burned in half, his innards gone in a burst of ash and nothing else. Shocked beyond words, I was unable to look away, unable to believe what I was seeing. What happened to Salamanders being immune to the heat of fire and lava?

But more importantly, what was Fiametta hiding that would make her go against her own decree? Something she was willing to give up a traitor and his connections, a lover she'd held in her arms, to protect.

Peta's eyes met mine and I put a hand on her head. "Thanks."

"That's four times now, Terraling."

I swallowed hard. "I think you'll get at least a few more chances to pull my ass from the fire before we're out of here."

She bobbed her head. "I believe you may be right."

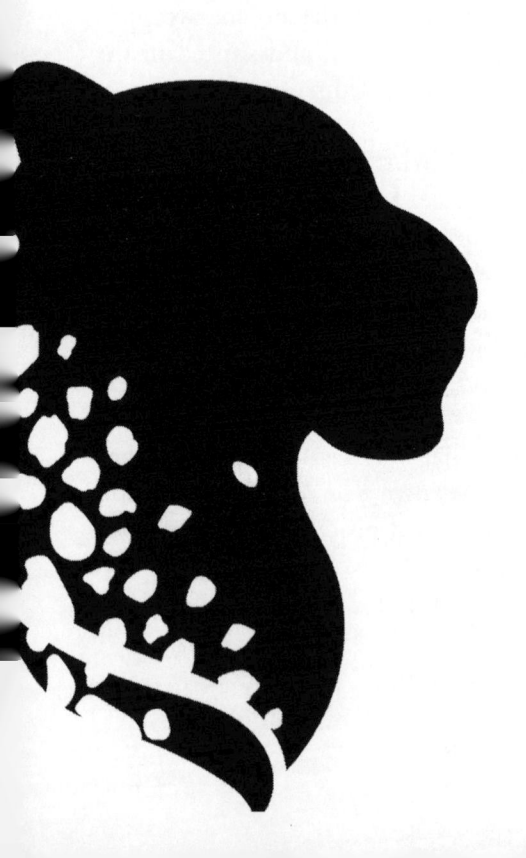

Chapter 10

Peta stayed crouched over me, as the lava in the air receded like a wave pulled out to sea. "Be wary, Dirt Girl. The queen is most dangerous when she is scared. And I believe she is terrified."

I rolled to my back and found myself looking up at the queen. Her blue eyes stared down at me, but it was the two high spots on her cheeks that told me Peta was right. They were the only sign of emotion I'd seen on her.

I started to get up but she held a hand over me, the palm shimmering with a red glow. "Do not move, Terraling. How did you know he was a traitor?"

Worm shit and green sticks, there was no way I could tell her about my ability with Spirit. Not if Cactus was right about the way she used people. I swallowed hard.

From Peta came a single word reverberating through me. *Lie.*

But lies had a way of being outed so I went with the closest thing to the truth I could. "He bragged about it to someone else when I was supposed to be unconscious. That he was bedding you while he searched for 'it.'"

Her eyes narrowed. "And how did you know about his hand, and the scar? He rarely takes his gloves off."

Unless he was in bed with her were the unspoken words. Which of course would mean I'd spied on them during the act. Which I had, though it wasn't my fault.

Under my back, the smooth stone slowly heated, as if the lava below was picking up on the queen's mood. Not a good sign.

Cactus cleared his throat and the queen's gaze swung to the left. "You have something to tell me, Cactus?"

"Yes, my queen. Lark told me what she'd heard, and we were going to speak to Brand about it. Lark didn't know who the scar belonged to." Which didn't answer how I'd seen it, but maybe the diversion would work.

Peta, quiet through all the talk, slowly put herself between Fiametta and me, as the tension continued to rise. Fiametta was no fool, that much was clear.

I swallowed hard, but otherwise didn't move. Fiametta turned to me, the heat from her hand directly over my heart. "Who was he speaking to?"

"I don't know. I only heard him speak and saw him scratch at his scar before I blacked out again."

Her eyes narrowed to mere slits. "And you didn't think you were dreaming?"

"I know what I heard." I took a chance, one that would either put her at ease or make her kill me right there. I sat up, which put her hand right in front of my face. "Fiametta, you're friends with Cassava. You should know better than anyone that as part of the Rim, I can say I know the difference between dreams and reality with absolute clarity."

She lowered her hand, but continued to stare down at me, her face unreadable. "Yes, I suppose you would have to learn that if you want to survive in her family."

Her family. Like Cassava still ruled the Rim. I itched to put Fiametta to the question. To ask her all she knew about Cassava and the bitch's plans. Almost as much as that, I wanted to know what was hidden in her room. Something she was willing to kill someone she cared about in order to keep hidden.

The queen of the Pit took a step back. "You willingly stepped in front of me when I would have otherwise been attacked. For that I will give you credit."

"I saved your life," I said. "Give me Ash's, surely your life is worth that of a simple Ender who you have no care for."

Peta let out a barely audible hiss. "Too far."

I pushed to my feet and dusted my clothes off. Too far it might have been, but I had to ask. I had to push if I was to save Ash's life.

Fiametta laughed and I was surprised at the soft tones of it. A real laugh, one not hidden behind the mask of royalty. "You think so? I do not. As queen, my life is not worth more than those of my Enders, nor any of my people. I would lay down my life for any of them, Terraling."

Her words stopped me. Maybe she wasn't as much like Cassava as I'd been thinking.

"Then you won't give him even a measure of mercy?"

"No. Four lives were taken at his hands. Four. At best, I could credit him a single life, except I was still forced to take the life of yet another Ender, one who also filled a spot in my bed." She lifted an eyebrow, her lips quirking upward at the edges. "Unless perhaps you'd like to take his place?"

"As an Ender for the Pit?" I was confused and struggled to understand until she gave me a soft smile, her eyes sparkling with humor and desire.

Oh shit. I'd thought the thing about her libido was exaggerated. Apparently not so much.

I gave her a bow from the waist. "Thank you, but I do believe I will have to forgo your offer. I am only here for three days after all."

Her face closed off and she inclined her head. "You know more than you say, and I believe there is more to you than you let on—"

"I am an Ender," I said softly. "Nothing else. I will do what I must to protect those in my care. No matter who they are."

Her eyes went cold again, and I knew I'd struck a chord I hadn't meant to.

"You may visit your friend once. That is the gift I offer you for placing your life in front of mine." She turned and strode toward the entrance Cactus had collapsed. He scrambled to get it open for her, lifting the rock and pushing it all to one side. The queen never looked back, and I realized just how scared I'd been facing her. My legs shook and I had to lock my knees to keep them from buckling.

Peta shrunk to her housecat form and she trotted to my side. "Dirt Girl, what are you doing, turning the queen down? When she beckons you to her bed, you go!"

I snorted. "Flattered as I was, I cannot fake desire."

"If you want to survive the Pit, perhaps you'd best learn how to 'fake' it, as you say," she grumbled at me. I scooped her up and kissed her on the nose.

"Peta, I love you."

"Gah, put me down, Terraling!"

"You see?" I let her down. "I cannot fake it."

Brand took a few steps after the queen, then turned and looked at me. "Peta is right, no one turns down the queen."

I arched an eyebrow at him. "Not even you?"

"Not even me." There was sadness and regret in his eyes. I thought about Smoke, about her having to share him with their beautiful, but-oh-so-deadly, queen.

"Perhaps if more people stood up to her, she wouldn't be such a power hungry bitch." Yet even as I said the words, I realized that wasn't the case. She'd shown that she placed her life on par with all her people's lives. Though it did not help Ash any, I could give her credit that she at least didn't set her life above theirs.

And then I realized I'd lost my one bargaining chip. The traitor was dead, and I was no further ahead in getting Ash out of the Pit. Damn it to the seven hells and back.

I made my decision quickly. "She said I could see Ash."

"No, not yet," Brand said. I bent and picked up my spear, twisting it in half and hanging it from my belt in two pieces.

"Two questions, Brand." I crossed my arms and lifted an eyebrow at him. "Why can I not see him now, and where the hell did you get my spear?"

"Your spear was sent by your father. And you can't see Ash because he is healing."

My father . . . my brain struggled to comprehend. "My father sent my spear. And you let me have it?"

And then the second half of what Brand said hit home, and I stepped toward him, hands dropping into fists. "What do you mean he is healing?"

Brand shrugged. "Ash started a fight with one of the other prisoners. So he's a bit bruised up. As to your father, here, he sent a note with the spear. It got here just a few moments before I saw you on the ledge up here. You can have it only because I am vouching for you. Again. Use it on anyone and I will be in the dungeons with you."

"Why would you do that?"

"You just pulled a traitor down and you've been here for less than a day. You tell me why I'm trusting you." He pulled a sealed envelope from inside his black leather top and handed it to me. The seal was green wax with a perfect blooming tree imprint. I ran a thumb over it, fear filling me. Without opening it, I tucked it into my vest. "Thank you. For this and for trusting me."

Brand nodded. "Lark, you have done as I asked and ousted the traitor. Now I must hold to my end of the bargain. Ash wanted to get you out of here. You've seen just how dangerous the Pit is. And now you have sparked the interest of the queen. Please, reconsider—"

"No, I'm staying until either I get Ash out or . . ." my guts tightened as I realized I might not be able to save him. I might be staying to watch him die and be a final witness to his sacrifice for me. My throat burned and filled with a thick lump. I had to swallow several times to force it down. "Or the three days is up," I finally managed. Then there was the issue of the firewyrms. They were being killed off and I had to do something; I felt it in the core of my bones that I couldn't leave them to Fiametta's culling.

Brand's eyes softened and lifted his hand as if to pat me on the shoulder. My jaw twitched and he must have seen something in my eyes because he withdrew his hand. "The sleep bell will ring soon. Go." He turned and went down the stairs closest to us without another word.

"Cactus—"

My friend took my hand and led me away, and I let him.

"He's right, Lark. We need to get back to my place before we pass out in the halls."

The thought of sleeping and unable to wake in one of the myriad of labyrinthine hallways gave me a chill I did not like. Still, I pulled my hand from his.

"And I suppose you're going to tell me we need to leave without Ash too?"

Cactus laughed. "No, if you still have the heart of the girl I grew up with, I know we aren't leaving without Ash. One way or another. But with the traitor dead, what other option do you have? Do you have another way to save Ash?"

In that moment I loved him more than a little. He didn't try to sway me from my chosen course of action, but backed me.

That didn't mean I had any sort of idea what I was going to do. Climbing up the stairs that had taken us to the edge of the Pit, it didn't take long for my legs to feel the strain. It reminded me of my Ender training, which, while it seemed a lifetime ago, had been less than six months past.

My teacher had been Granite, a man I'd trusted, respected and thought was my friend. It turned out that not only was he not my friend, he was actively trying to wipe out my family alongside Cassava. Still, a part of me wished I could ask him what to do. He'd been an Ender long before I'd been born, and even though he'd been a traitor to my father, he was known for his brilliant tactics. So far I'd managed to survive both Cassava's treachery and the dark secrets within the Deep, but both times had been based on strength and fighting ability more than anything else.

There was nothing here for me to physically fight; I needed to outsmart these Salamanders within their own home. And I wasn't sure I could do it.

Peta trotted at my side and I glanced down at her. The sight of her white tipped tail made me smile despite the hard situation at hand. I realized I had the perfect helper if she would open to me. Living in the Pit as a familiar, surely she would have an idea as to how to save Ash? I just didn't know if she would trust me enough to help me. Her antagonism was not exactly subtle even though she was softening toward me.

The three of us remained silent as we emerged from the downward tunnel into the main living quarters cavern. Cactus walked me back to Smoke and Brand's home. He stopped in front of the open door, leaning against the edge of it. "I'd take you with me, but people might talk." He gave me a slow wink.

I snorted, opened my mouth to respond when his eyes widened as he looked over my shoulder. Damn these Salamanders and their penchant for creeping around in complete silence. I arched an eyebrow at Cactus and he gave a slight shake of his head. So whoever was behind me was no one I wanted to talk to apparently. Keeping my back to whomever, I spoke to them. "Sneaking up on people? Isn't that below you?"

A sharp intake of breath and then a fist jammed between my shoulder blades, throwing me forward. I spun as I fell, catching a glimpse of bright red curls.

Maggie glared down at me. "I'm here to make sure you do as told. The queen thinks Brand is going soft."

"Or maybe you asked for this duty? A reason to push me around?" I stood and didn't bother to hide my anger. With that emotion running through me I could truly tap into the earth's power and feel as though I could hold my own against any other elemental. I let the anger burn bright, feeding it with the fact Maggie had been the first to stand against me and Ash when we'd come for help.

"If you'd helped us when we asked, instead of fighting us, we could have been in and out of the Pit without anyone even knowing, Maggie. None of this would have happened. No one would have died."

Maggie glared at me. "If you had taken our advice and left, no one would have died."

"My whole family would have!" I shouted at her, unable to contain the words in any sort of moderation.

She snorted. "And the world would have been a better place for that."

Several gasps around us told me I was not the only one who thought she'd gone too far.

Maggie's hands glowed a soft red as she called on her element and I watched closely as a tiny flame burst into life over the top of her hand. She rolled it over her knuckles, the fire dancing across her skin. "You're going to die here, Larkspur. It won't matter that your father is the king of the Rim, or that you're an Ender. It won't matter that you saved the queen."

Cactus stepped around me and the colors that swirled up his arms blended green and red twinning about one another as the tiny rocks at our feet slowly rose in the air. "Do not threaten her, Maggie."

Maggie laughed and put her hands on her hips, the fire dancing from her hands to race around the edge of her body. "Being a tad over dramatic, aren't we? I'm not killing her. Yet."

I lifted a hand to Cactus, ignoring her. "Thanks for showing me around."

I turned my back on Maggie. She snarled and I dodged to the right as she crashed toward me, the flash of black leathers my only warning. She clipped my shoulder, spinning me into the house and against a long pair of legs. I looked up into Smoke's eyes.

"Lark, what is going on?"

"Maggie's lost it," I spit out.

Maggie grabbed my ankles and dragged me out of the house before I could say anything else.

"Maggie, stop this!" Smoke cried out.

Maggie tightened her grip on me and picked up speed. "No, I lost rank because of her and I'm about to fix that."

I had no idea what she was talking about, but I suspected that "fixing" things would mean a beating for me, or worse.

She had me out of the house, and was running backward as she dragged me along the open ground. The rough footing tore at my vest and pants, tearing at the few spots where my skin hit. And then I realized where she was dragging me.

The river of lava.

Oh, that was not happening. I jerked both legs at the same time, snapping my knees against my chest, which pulled Maggie toward me, her orange eyes wide with surprise.

I tipped my head forward as she inadvertently launched up my body, and her forehead crashed into the top of mine. The reverberation from the impact shuddered down my spine and my shoulder gave a distant twinge, but I was no longer playing nice. I rolled with Maggie as her eyes widened with shock. Grabbing her by the shoulders as I straddled her waist, I thumped her hard into the ground, anger slicing through any hesitation I might have had.

Two more times I slammed her into the ground, her head bouncing with enough force that I almost felt bad. Almost.

I let her go and stood, breathing hard so it took me a moment to realize there was an eerie silence in the air. Around me were other fire elementals, their strange eyes in every shade of orange and yellow imaginable staring at me with nothing short of fear.

A few of them clung to their powers, the red lines licking up their arms indicating how close they were to blasting me. I slowly lifted my hands, feeling the weight of every move I made. "She started it."

"You are a guest here," Smoke's voice was soft but with an edge. A rebuke if I ever heard it.

"And if she'd gotten me to the lava flow? Would any of you have stopped her?" Many of the Salamanders looked away, their eyes dropping. "That's what I thought. Don't expect that I won't defend myself."

The crowd dispersed, although more than one Salamander looked over their shoulder at me. The dislike reminded me strongly of Peta's own distaste for me and apparently all Terralings.

Turning, I looked for Cactus. He was walking away, too, taking an unconscious Maggie with him. And he didn't look back. A sigh slipped out of me and Smoke touched my shoulder gently.

"You are right, you have to defend yourself, but in front of so many people? That will not help you or your friend." She shook her head, her eyes sorrowful. "Come, eat."

Peta gave a meow and I instinctively held out my arms. She leapt up and worked her way up to my shoulder. "You should have smashed her at least twice more."

I startled and looked up at the cat. "You aren't going to tell me I should have let her pulverize me?"

She snorted and shook her head. "No, showing weakness in the Pit will get you killed. The others fear you now; they saw you beat Maggie's ass in a matter of seconds. That is why she came at you. You've beaten her once and she lost standing, losing to a mere Dirt Girl. Now you've beaten her a second time. She will look for another way to get at you. So we will have to be extra vigilant."

I wished I could believe Peta that I'd done the right

thing. Maybe in some ways I had, but I knew one thing for sure. No matter what happened, Maggie and I would never be friends.

CHAPTER 11

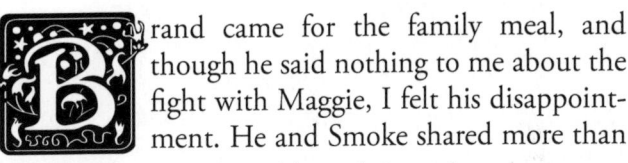

Brand came for the family meal, and though he said nothing to me about the fight with Maggie, I felt his disappointment. He and Smoke shared more than one glance across the table and their three boys were remarkably quiet. Until the plates were cleared.

Tinder shifted in his seat. "Did you really beat up Maggie?"

I looked from the boy to his father.

Brand leaned back and crossed his arms over his chest. "Go ahead. Tell him."

Peta looked up from my lap, her green eyes unblinking. "Yes, tell him."

Putting my hands on the table edge, I nodded.

"Yes, I knocked her out. She came at me from behind." Maybe that would be enough.

Tinder's eyes widened and his tiny mouth opened into a perfect *O*. "And you *still* beat her?"

Peta stretched, her back arching into a perfect curve as she stepped off my lap and onto the table. "Terralings are not to brag. They're humble, unlike you lizards."

Brand seemed to be holding back a smile as Peta crossed the table. Smoke glowered but only for a second.

Peta pushed up onto her back two legs, front paws stretched into the air. "Magma leapt at her from behind and the Dirt Girl sensed it coming. She rolled with Magma tackling her. And *BAM*! the first punch smashed its target." The cat dropped to all fours and rolled over then popped into the air to land flat on her belly. Apparently my familiar was a natural born storyteller.

"What happened next?" Tinder whispered, his tiny fists pressed under his chin.

Peta dragged herself across the table with her front claws, weaving one way and then the other. "Magma raced backward, dragging the Terraling by her ankles. Right to the lava flow."

Tinder gasped and his fists shook with suppressed emotion. "What then?"

Peta slithered on her belly until she was hidden behind one of the dishes. "It looked as though Magma would throw her into the lava flow. But the Terraling used her legs, jerking Magma off balance, cracking their heads against one another."

"And because she is a Terraling her skull is harder than Magma's?" Tinder asked and Peta rolled onto her back and jabbed her four feet into the air as if in a four-legged boxing match.

"Exactly." She paused and rolled into attack position, her body wiggling with suppressed movement. "The Dirt Girl grabbed Magma by the shoulders and slammed her against the ground three times." Peta's head bobbed up and down. "*BAM BAM BAM*. Each time harder than the last until she was satisfied Magma would not be coming around anytime soon." At the last second, Peta leapt toward Tinder, landing right in front of his face. He squealed and laughed and she sat and looked over her shoulder at me.

I shook my head. "You see, that is not much at all."

Stryker grinned at me. "That's huge. Maggie is a tough Ender. Dad always says so, and now you've beaten her twice. I'd watch my back. She'll want another go at you." His words echoing what Peta had already cautioned.

"Wonderful," I muttered.

Smoke clapped her hands. "Boys, off to bed. The bell will ring soon." The three boys scrambled up and I was surprised as each of them went by me, touching two fingers to the top of their opposite hand, and then repeating the gesture to the top of mine.

I waited until they were gone deeper into the house before I lifted an eyebrow at Brand. "What was that about?"

"They were showing their respect for you. Touching your hand like that is acknowledging that you have more power than them." His eyes dropped and he let out a yawn. "Don't expect it from me, though."

I laughed but it was forced. I let Smoke lead me to a simply made-up room that looked comfortable. The bed was bigger than the one I had in our Enders Barracks, the thin, pale-blue silk sheets beckoning. My body craved sleep despite the rest I'd had at Cactus's place.

Thanking Smoke, I waited for her to leave before I sat on the edge of the bed. Peta sat at my feet, reached up with her front paws and dug them into the bed then stretched her back. She cracked a yawn. "The bell is coming."

"I need to stay awake," I said, looking straight into the light tube that lit my room. By the color of the light, I figured time was closing on the night. "I have to find a way to get Ash out of here and I only have two days left."

Peta pulled herself onto the bed beside me. "And you think you can withstand the bell when it rings? No one stays awake. The mother goddess herself would have to help you withstand the sleep bell."

"So be it then. I will ask her."

With everyone else asleep, the night was the perfect time to search. Besides, if Peta was right, how did the Ender Coal stay awake to search the Queen's chambers? How had the queen woken when she'd heard him? If they could stay awake, then there was no reason I couldn't either.

I knelt on the floor and placed my hands on the solid stone underneath me. Breathing out slowly, I tried to form the right words, the ones that would bring the mother goddess to me.

A deep booming gong sounded, like thunder rolling over clear blue skies. The echo hit my body like a physical blow and I gasped. "Mother goddess, I must stay awake."

The power of Spirit will protect you, child. You do not need me.

Her voice was a soothing balm over my fears and I sat quietly as three more booms echoed through the Pit. Beside me Peta snorted. "Damn, you truly are a child of Spirit, aren't you?"

"How do you know this? How do you know anything about Spirit?"

She hesitated and I saw the struggle in her as she tried to fight the urge to help me more than she had to. I felt her emotions, there, at the edge of my mind. Worry, regret, and uncertainty.

I put a hand on her back as gently as I could. "I won't share your secrets, Peta."

Her eyes flicked to mine then away. "My first charge,

years ago, was a child of Spirit. I am the last familiar that ever watched over one such as you. I believe that is why the mother goddess assigned me as your familiar."

A breath I didn't realize I'd been holding whooshed out of me. "You really can help me then."

"I think so." The uncertainty was there again. "But you must understand, he was fully trained when I was given to him as a kitten. I know what he was capable of, but I don't know *how* he did what he did."

Without thinking, I scooped her up and pressed my face against her. I hadn't realized how much fear I'd carried about that part of me until Peta said she could guide me. I held her with my eyes closed and she purred.

"I'm so glad you are here," I whispered. "No matter what happens."

Her rough tongue flicked once over my cheek. "So am I, Dirt Girl. But if you tell anyone, I will claw your face to ribbons while you sleep."

Smiling, I shifted her to my shoulder, her claws digging into the leather vest for balance.

I knew where I wanted look first. Smoke's earlier words were my only clue to go on. "Peta, we need to go to the healer's rooms."

"Are you ill?" The concern in her voice and the feeling of worry coursing through her into me was touching.

"No, I just . . . I need to see where the Enders were treated. Where they died. There could be a clue as to what happened to them."

She tipped her chin forward. "Then let us go."

Opening my door, I listened for a moment. The home was quiet and I crept out, stopping in the main room to grab my spear. With my luck, I would need it, even though everyone was asleep.

Creeping into the main cavern, the weight of the silence

was like a living breathing boogey man that waited in the shadows. The light tubes dulled to a dim glow with only the moon's light reflecting through the mountain to us, giving the place a strange iridescence.

Peta sniffed the air. "I've never been awake at night inside the mountain, it feels different."

"Like something is waiting for us," I said and her claws dug in tightly.

"Dirt Girl. Those are not words you want to utter out loud."

I thought of Scar and wondered how many of the firewyrms were left.

I broke into a jog, heading for the bridge, the lava bubbling happily under it. "Why not?"

"There are creatures in the Pit that even the queen would not face. Beasts from long ago that sleep under the lava."

"Like the firewyrms."

"Yes, like them. And others. Others I have never had the displeasure of meeting. Creatures that would make the Deep seem a playground and the Rim like Heaven."

"Lovely."

We reached the bridge and hurried across, the heat chasing me. My skin was dry to the point of tiny cracks appearing across it. Soon they would break open and bleed as they begged for moisture. Thoughts of the Deep emerged and suddenly going back didn't seem like that much of a hardship.

"Take this opening." Peta flicked one paw as if shaking off droplets of water. I jogged into the cavern hallways and came to a sudden halt. The hallways that had been lit during the day were dark, not one embedded flame in the wall, not one flicker of fire to show us the way.

"Peta, how well can you see in the dark?"

"I need at least a glimmer. Even I cannot see in total darkness."

I backed into the main cavern. We weren't far from the singles quarters. "Cactus might have something we can use, a torch perhaps."

Peta nodded and I ran toward his home. Cactus's place was easy to find with all the junk and garbage surrounding it. I pushed a few things around with my feet looking for something that would work as a torch before giving up on my search and going into his house. The plants growing around us leaned in toward me. I lifted a hand to a young bamboo plant shooting out of the ground. If I stuffed the end with a bit of cloth, it would work for a torch.

"Forgive me," I whispered as I took my spear and cut the bamboo at the ground. It would grow back, but even so, I didn't take lightly to cutting it down. Searching through Cactus's place for some fabric or cloth, I found myself at his bedroom door.

Peta shook her head, her eyes catching mine. "Don't go in there, Dirt Girl. You won't like it."

As if that would make me walk away. I slowly pushed the door open. Cactus was sprawled on his bed, his naked torso raising and falling with his deep breaths. I sucked in a sharp breath.

Beside him lay Maggie, her riotous curls spread over his pillow, and her body also naked, her armor spread over the floor as if it had been taken off and dropped where she stood.

"Shit," I whispered even though I knew they wouldn't wake. "I didn't mean to beat up his girlfriend."

Which explained why he hadn't looked back when he'd left. I refused to feel anything, refused to acknowledge it hurt my feelings that he would sleep with Maggie of all people. I bent and grabbed one of his shirts from the floor and wrapped it around the end of the bamboo. A small part of me hoped it was one of his favorites.

"Are you upset, Dirt Girl?" Peta asked.

"Why would I be upset?" Why indeed? I had no claim on him other than friendship.

"Because he kissed you today and I feel how much you care for him. This is a betrayal. Why does it not bother you?"

"And I have kissed Ash. Neither of them are my bedmates, play mates, or anything between those. Friends, that is all." The words came out a little harsher than I'd planned and I let out a breath. "Okay, maybe it bothers me a little, but I can't be surprised. Cactus lives here, this is his home."

"But he wants to escape," she pointed out.

I left Cactus and Maggie sleeping peacefully and headed back the way we'd come. "Yes, he does. That doesn't mean he won't enjoy what is left of his stay here."

I went to the bridge and stood at the edge, dipping the torch close to the rolling river of liquid death. Before the material even touched the surface, it burst into flames. Stepping back, I held the torch aloft and went to the opening. Stepping into the darkness, the torch didn't throw the light as far as I would have liked but Peta gave a chirping sound.

"I can see. But your torch won't last so we must hurry."

Knowing she was right I broke into a slow jog, taking the turns and twists as Peta directed until I stood in front of the healer's rooms. She took us on a direct route, and the rooms weren't as far away as they'd seemed when others had led us.

The rod of Asclepius etched into the double doors glittered in the torchlight. Under the flickering flame, the snake looked far more like a firewyrm than any other reptile, now that I'd met a firewyrm in person. I slowed and put my hand on the door, half expecting it to be locked. But it opened easily and I stepped inside, shutting the door quickly. Setting the torch into a wall scone, I peered around me, taking the place in.

The room was empty of patients, and clean of any blood that may have been spilled. Around the edge of the room, a counter was built into the wall, and on it were tools of the healer's trade. Scalpels, knives, ointments, and herbals for a variety of ailments, bandages, wraps, and splints set aside, ready at a moment's notice. But none of that was what I needed.

"Where would they put those who are critically injured? And would they have taken notes?" I placed a hand on one of the empty beds, leaning on it.

Peta hopped from my shoulder and trotted around the room, sniffing. "I don't know. What are we looking for?"

That was the question I wasn't sure I had an answer to. I cupped the back of my neck with my hands. "I don't know exactly. Evidence of some sort."

"That is not helpful, Dirt Girl."

"Just see if anything sticks out to you." I walked around the room, touching the jars of herbs and salves, ointments for burns mostly. Which was interesting. "Why do so many Salamanders get burned when they are immune to the flames?"

"Normally they don't but lately there have been injuries of that kind for many of them. Usually the salves are saved for those who are visiting the Pit," Peta jumped onto the counter that ran around the entire room, putting her nose into several jars, sneezing in one.

Her nose twitched. "Occasionally a death occurs because a child who is too young tries to swim in the lava."

I shuddered. "Why would they let them do that?"

"They don't. These are children in their early teenage years who believe they are invincible." Peta's voice grew sad. "One of my charges was just such a child."

Gut wrenching grief flowed from Peta into me and I had to clamp down on the tears that threatened. Tears that would burn my face with their heat and the remembrance of my own loss.

"Peta—"

"Shhhh." She hissed, her eyes narrowing and her ears twitching. "Hide. Someone is coming."

Chapter 12

Worm shit and green sticks. I scrambled for one of the beds, sliding under it with far more noise than was good. The butt of my spear bounced off the floor and I grabbed it, pulling it tight to my side as the door creaked open. A tiny figure cloaked in a dark material from head to foot slipped in; the very same one I'd seen at the edge of the river.

Whoever she was, she would have barely come up to the top of my breasts, so maybe five feet tall at best. Other than that, I could see no distinguishing features. If she *was* Cassava, she'd found a way to hide her height as well as her features. Whoever she was, she hid behind a spell that cloaked her, hiding her. This was no ghost, no specter.

She crept through the healer's room to the counter where the healing balms were and grabbed a jar of ointment. Spinning around she searched the room and I held my breath.

"Who is here? I can sense you." The voice was wavy and distorted and I couldn't tell if they were even male or female. If it hadn't been for Smoke's belief it was a girl, I wasn't sure I would have thought that.

She took a few steps toward me and I lay there, thinking that she was about the right size to be Finley. But what the hell would the Queen of the Deep be doing sneaking around the Pit? No, Finley would never stoop to this kind of behavior.

A few more steps and she was at the edge of the bed. Even her feet were cloaked in shadows. I had to give it to her, it was a disguise worth learning.

Peta gave out a high-pitched meow and trotted along the edge of the counter, drawing the attention away from me. The cloaked one spun and stared.

"Damn cats. I hate felines. The first thing I'll do when I rule the Pit as queen is kill all you snotty creatures."

Well, now I knew for sure she was a she. Though not a nice girl, that was obvious. Peta let out a long low hiss, her fur standing on end. But she didn't say anything and the mystery girl slipped out of the healer's room as quietly as she'd entered. I stayed where I was for another minute before I crawled out.

"Peta, did you—"

"No, I could not even get a scent on her, whatever spell covers her, it is complete. It makes no sense, there are no young rivals for the throne here." She shook her head.

"Did you see what ointment she took?" Already my mind leapt forward. We could be on the lookout for someone who had whatever injury the girl was trying to heal.

"Burn salve," Peta said.

I nodded, and debated going after the girl. "That is no ghost." I stopped and shook my head. "Keep looking, maybe we can still find something solid."

"Unless you have an idea of what it is you are looking for, I will not keep sniffing jars." Peta yawned, her tiny jaws cracking wide as she flashed her teeth and rough tongue at me.

I crouched beside her. "I attacked four Enders when I was here, all the injuries were bad, but the two worst happened right here. As soon as I hurt them, the healers were helping them. How could they have died when they had healers—the best in our world—right here?"

Peta's eyes widened as she caught what I was getting at. "If someone wanted to see you go down in flames, they would only have to make sure the Enders didn't survive."

"Exactly. But I have to prove it." And therein lay the rub. We scoured the room, top to bottom three times over but found nothing out of the ordinary. Until I opened the second to last cupboard. Inside were stacks of paper, labeled with names.

"Peta."

She ran to my side, putting her paws on my knee as I crouched. "They would be the most recent, no one has died since then."

I grabbed the top four pieces of paper.

Name: Ender Blaze
Injury: Spear wound to lateral oblique, three ribs broken.
Treatment: Stitches, binding for the ribs, heavy dose of herbals for pain.
Prognosis: Stable, good condition.

Name: Ender Flare

Injury: Spear wound to neck, artery cut.
Treatment: Stitches, infusion of blood, heavy dose of herbals for pain.
Prognosis: Stable, good condition.

Name: Ender Smudge
Injury: Spear wound to stomach.
Treatment: Stitches, loose wrap, heavy dose of herbals for pain.
Prognosis: Stable, good condition.

Name: Ender Stokes
Injury: Spear wound to stomach.
Treatment: Stitches, loose wrap, heavy dose of herbals for pain.
Prognosis: Stable, good condition.

I flipped each of the papers over, seeing the times the healers checked on each of them. "Everything here shows they were all healing, in good spirits," I whispered.

Peta tapped the paper with a paw. "Until the end."

The final line on each paper was simple. DOMC.

"Dead on morning check." She translated for me.

"Peta, will this help? Will Fiametta even look at this?" And in the back of my head I wondered why the healers hadn't shown these papers to their queen.

She wrinkled up her nose. "It's hard to say. Maybe. It's your best shot, I think."

I folded the papers, sliding them under my vest. My fingers brushed against the letter from my father. I still had to read that too, but I was reluctant. A part of me was afraid to see what exactly he had to say.

The torchlight flickered and I glanced over my shoulder.

The bamboo was burnt more than halfway down and Cactus's shirt was long gone.

"Peta, we're running out of time." I grabbed a spool of cloth from the counter top, bandages folded up and ready for an emergency. I wrapped them around the torch hoping to stave off the inevitable.

"Hurry up, Dirt Girl. If you don't want to be found here, then we have to leave." She ran ahead of me and nudged the door open with her face. I tightened my grip on the torch and took one last look back into the room. I only had to prove the Enders didn't die as a result of my spear. Injured? Yes, that much I would admit to, but no longer did I feel the weight of their deaths. The papers proved I was not their killer.

Peta ran ahead of me, the tip of her tail a flashing white spot in the darkness. The torch burnt lower, the heat scorching my hand as I took another turn. "Peta, how much farther?"

"A few minutes."

"We aren't going to make it." The torch took that moment to burn my hand, sizzling the skin and forcing me to drop it. The glowing embers littered the floor and Peta ran back to me.

"Looks like we're sleeping here," I said.

"No, we can't. If they find you out of Smoke and Brand's home, it is the excuse they will use to throw you into jail next to Ash." Peta spoke quickly and I let out a groan.

I crouched beside her, her green eyes glowing in the last of the light. "Could you find your way out now that we are this close?"

"Yes, but I must be on the ground to smell."

I nodded and the last of the embers burned out dropping us into a total and complete darkness that was not comfortable in the least. "Call out to me, Peta. I'll follow your voice."

"Got it. This way." Her voice echoed to me and I took a few steps forward, my hand on the wall for guidance. I came to an opening, and I grasped the edge of it.

"Peta?"

"This way, Larkspur." Her voice came from the right and I turned, following her instructions. Turn after turn and ten minutes turned into fifteen. I paused at the next intersection. "Peta, how much farther?"

There was no response and I swallowed hard. "Peta?"

A low rumbling laugh echoed through the darkness. "So easy to deceive, little Larkspur. So easy to lead astray. Your familiar is already out of the tunnels and here you are, lost deep within the Pit."

I flattened my back against the wall and slid away from the intersection. "Who are you?"

"You don't recognize me? You should."

My eyes strained in the darkness, seeing things that weren't there, flashes of light that were just my mind trying to fill in the utter black. Immediately I thought of the tiny cloaked figure. Twice now I'd seen her and the voice was similar enough, that it could have been her. Or maybe someone cloaking themselves just like her. Smoke said there were two specters. Was I meeting the second?

"No, I don't recognize you. But then, I rarely waste my time with tricksters," I said as I slid away from the intersection, back the way I'd come.

"Oh, I am not a trickster, but I do know who killed those Enders. You want to know that secret, don't you?" Damn it, the voice was everywhere, in front to the left and the right. But that was impossible.

Unless maybe it was someone from the supernatural

world; a warlock maybe, or worse yet, a demon. I'd not dealt with the supernatural world, but I'd learned about it as part of my schooling. The power of the elemental world ran in the supernatural bloodlines, giving them abilities they should not have.

I clung to the stone, a low spiral of fear keeping me far away from the anger I needed to tap into my powers. "Are you an elemental?"

"Yes, of course, dear Larkspur. Why would you ask that? Ahh, you think me supernatural in nature. Good guess, but that isn't what you face."

That left only one possibility: he had to be a Spirit user. There was no other answer to the way I felt, the way I'd heard Peta calling me the wrong way, farther into the tunnels. It was a trick Cassava used when she wore the pink diamond, a stone that gave her the powers of a Spirit user.

There was no way this trickster knew I had that same element running through my veins. I reached out for the part of me that held Spirit and clung to it, wrapping it around me. The warmth sunk through my soul and the fear and confusion slipped away. Holding my breath, I dropped to my knees. If I couldn't see him, then I doubted he could see me. At least that was what I was hoping for.

Spirit didn't require me to be angry to tap into it, not like my powers that were connected to the earth. But that didn't mean Spirit was much help either since I didn't know what I was doing with it most times.

Crawling on my hands and knees, I tried to sense where he was, the way I'd felt Fiametta earlier in the day. Like a wolf scenting its prey, I crept forward. An image smashed into my skull of Griffin in full wolf form as he loped through the forest, his nose raised to the wind. My skin crawled as if the cool breeze actually coursed along my body.

"Whatever are you doing, dear Larkspur? I smell the Rim as if I stood under the redwoods." His voice was no longer confident, but had an edge of irritation to it.

But better yet, his voice no longer rebounded and his words echoed from the left. Pushing myself to the tips of my toes and creeping across the floor on my hands and toe tips, I approached him. A sudden pulse of his heart through the ground below froze me in place.

"Larkspur. Come out now," he snapped and a flicker of power danced over my skin. I realized he was trying to compel me with Spirit. A grin spread over my lips and I was sure that if he could see it, he would run for his life.

Whoever this was, I was going to catch him and shake him 'til he spilled his secrets. I scurried forward, my back hunched and my steps silent. The sound of his breathing, the sound of his heart beating was loud in my ears. I leapt toward him, a howl on my lips as Griffin's wolf spirit seemed to channel through me.

He cried out and stumbled backward, screaming. "No!"

We tumbled to the floor and his hands seemed to be everywhere, punching and hitting . . . and sliding under my vest.

With a quick snatch he had the papers along with the note from my father. "I don't think you'll be needing these."

Rotten worm shit, how had he known? He had to have been spying on me in the healer's room.

We rolled and he got loose. I didn't stop fighting to gain a hold on him, but still I missed him by an inch, the soft material of his clothing brushing my arm and sliding through my fingers as if water. He took off running in the utter darkness. I didn't hesitate to bolt after him. Holding tight to the pulse of his life in the back of my head, the reverberation of his feet on the stone as he ran I tracked him as easily as if I could see him in front of me.

Pumping my arms and legs hard, I closed the distance between us with each stride until his long cloak was tickling at my hands. He took a hard left and I followed but when I turned the corner, he was gone. As if he'd never been and I'd been chasing shadows.

"Son of a fey bitch in heat." I slapped my hands against the wall and the mountain gave a low rumble in response. Breathing hard, I leaned forward, knowing whoever he was, he wouldn't be gone long.

And whatever he was up to, no way it was good.

Other than losing him, I only had one pressing problem. Lifting my hands in front of me I fumbled forward, completely lost.

As a child, my mother always told me to sit down if I got lost, and someone would find me. Except I wasn't supposed to be out of the house, and I'd be damned if I was ending up in prison beside Ash. Again.

I didn't need to close my eyes to block out the darkness, but I needed to concentrate. There were only two people I could reach.

Cactus.

And Peta.

Swallowing hard I tried Peta first. When I concentrated, I could feel her emotions in the back of my head, her near panic as she searched for me poured through, and I struggled to breathe evenly. "Easy, Peta. I'm okay."

She didn't calm, but even worse, I couldn't truly reach her. I didn't understand the bond between us and how to use it fully.

"Damn." I rubbed my hands over my face and slid my

back down the wall. Dropping my hands to the floor I sent out a tiny pulse of energy, a call through the earth to Cactus. A call that would allow him to find me; if it could break through the sleep spell.

Licking my lips, a thought rolled through my brain. Maybe I could boost the call with Spirit, making Cactus hear me. A trick we'd used as children to reach one another, to sneak out at night and play under the stars.

I sent the call again, this time weaving Spirit around it. "Come on, Cactus."

That was all I could do. That and hope if Cactus didn't find me, Peta would. Or maybe Brand . . . anyone who wouldn't turn me over to the queen.

I closed my eyes again and slowed my breathing. There was nothing I could do now except wait.

In that silence, I reviewed the last few months of my life. Of the things I'd done and seen, and the truths I'd faced. The friends I'd gained and lost. "Mother goddess," I spoke into the darkness, "you said I was your chosen one. And you had me swear my life to you. For what? To bring me here and throw me into danger again?"

The weight of the darkness grew until the feeling of an arm rested across my shoulders and she whispered in my ear.

"Child, do you really want to know the future? Or would you rather live it and know each choice you make will take you to places you must be? Trust is a strange thing, so tied to fear. Let the fear go, Larkspur. Let it go, and trust not only yourself, but this world and the power of its elements."

The feeling of her arm receded and I stood, surprised to find my cheeks wet with tears. "Thank you."

There was a soft scuffle of claws on stone and a burst of flame broke through the darkness. Scar blinked up at me, his purple eyes dilated in the bright light. "You're lost, aren't you?"

I couldn't help the bitter laugh. "I am. Think you can help me back to the main cave?"

Scar nodded, and his fire went out. "Yes, just put a hand on me."

I touched the tip of one of his horns that arched over his neck. "Scar, how did you find me?"

"The mother goddess sent me. She said you will save us from Fiametta because you are the only one who can hear us speak." He moved forward, his gait a smooth side to side motion.

"Why is that, do you think?"

"I don't know, but the other Spirit Walker can't hear us. It is like he is deaf to our words."

I swallowed the sudden burst of excitement. "The other Spirit Walker? You mean the one in the cloak?"

"Yes, that is him. He made us do things ve did not want to. My father learned how to stop him, but now he steals us away." Scar let out a low sigh. "There aren't many of us left and . . ." He stopped speaking. "I must leave you here, Spirit Walker. Be careful there is much danger."

He flicked his head and I let go of his horn. "Thank you," I said into the darkness.

"Lark?"

I spun on as a torch flickered down the hallway. "Cactus?"

He jogged toward me but Peta blasting down the hallway caught my attention. Five feet away she leapt into my arms, her body shaking. "Lark, we have to go, right now."

"Yes, I know."

"No, you don't," Cactus said, his eyes strained at the edges. "Fiametta is on her way to Brand's, we saw her in the tunnels. We were just lucky she didn't see us."

Oh, that was not good in any way, shape, or form. "Then I guess we'd better get our asses in gear."

"You don't understand, Lark. We are all supposed to be asleep. And if you are not in your bed, asleep when she gets there. . ." He shook his head.

He didn't have to finish his sentence, I understood all too clearly.

If Fiametta had even an inkling I was doing what I shouldn't be, I would be toast; perhaps in the most literal sense of the word.

Chapter 13

Peta clung to me as Cactus ran ahead, the torchlight flickering. "Dirt Girl, who was that calling to you?"

I glanced at her then back to Cactus. "You heard him too?"

"Yes." Her claws dug into my clothes, the tops of them brushing against my skin. "I tried to stop you but you couldn't hear me and then . . . I couldn't find you." She shivered, her whole body twitching.

"I don't know who he is, but he can manipulate Spirit; he made it sound like you were calling to me."

Peta let out a low rumbling hiss. "But you stopped him?"

"For now. He took the papers."

She meowed softly in my ear. "He will be back, you think? We will get the papers from him then."

We took a hard left turn and I nodded. "I've no doubt about it." I had to believe hope was not lost.

Cactus slid to a stop and I almost slammed into him. "Why are we stopping?"

He pointed to a hole in the wall, the edges jagged and crumbling, the opening not very large. "Crawl through here. It will take you into a deserted home three doors down from Brand's place. Hurry."

I didn't question him, and neither did Peta. "Dirt Girl, go ahead of me this time, I don't want to lose you again."

Dropping to my knees I leaned into the opening and then lay flat on my belly as I shimmied forward. "How far?"

"Fifty feet."

"Wonderful," I muttered, pushing myself in. There wasn't a lot of room. It wasn't like I could really build up speed, but I had to try. Frantic to get to Brand's home ahead of Fiametta, I shoved myself along, my elbows and knees scraping in the dirt; my skin tearing open and filling with bits of rock. Sweat rolled down my face, and for the first time since I'd been in the Pit, it didn't evaporate right away. Which meant it acted as a perfect fluid for all the dust I stirred up to stick to me.

"Peta, she's going to know," I breathed into the shadowy darkness. Ahead of me there was a dim glow that had to be the way out.

"Just keep going. If you're in bed, she can't accuse you of being out."

"I'm covered in sweat and dirt; she isn't that blind."

"Dirt Girl, just go." She swiped a claw at my bare foot and I did as she said and concentrated on the exit. I fell through—finally—and quite literally. The tunnel opened four feet above the ground and I tumbled out, landing in a heap.

Peta leapt out after me and ran for the open door. She peered out and a low hiss escaped her. "Hurry, she is on the bridge."

Scrambling to my feet I lurched forward as I untangled my legs. Reaching the door, I took a quick look. Fiametta was at a distance, but no way would she miss me if making a run for it. If I could see her, she could most assuredly see me.

Pressing my back against the rock, I slid out the door toward Brand's home.

"Run, Dirt Girl," Peta snapped.

"If I run, her eyes will be drawn to me," I answered quietly. "You're a predator, surely you know that."

She snorted and then pressed herself against the wall. "I don't like when you're right."

"I don't like that you didn't argue she wasn't a predator." My back scraped along the wall, my heart hammered and my mind raced. We passed the first two homes with no problem, but Brand's home would be the clincher. I stood in the shadow of a low overhang between Brand's home and the one beside it.

"We need to distract her; find a way to get her to look behind her."

"Can you reach your earth powers?" Peta asked.

"If I'm angry enough." I looked across the cavern. With each moment that passed, the light grew and the shadow I hid in shrank.

"If you can do anything at all, now would be the time," Peta quipped. Damn it, she was right. I focused on Ash being locked away, on Fiametta and her games . . . but it didn't work. "Peta, help me out here."

"Cactus slept with Maggie after he kissed you," she said.

And there it was. A fierce hurt arched through me and I grabbed hold of the anger that flowed with it.

Behind Fiametta was the stone statue of the firewyrm that epitomized their family. I focused on it, thinking about how I'd broken down the sandstone doors in the Deep, and how shocked Requiem had been. Maybe that would work here too.

Pressing my hands into the ground, I pushed my power through the earth toward the statue. A wave of the earth rippled out from me—"Shit, she'll see where it came from," I growled.

Fiametta seemed oblivious to the wave until it hit the statue. The large obsidian fire lizard groaned as it rocked on its base. She turned and put her hands on her hips. The two Enders flanking her turned also; this was the moment I needed. I urged my power into the stone, finding the particles and pulling them apart bit by bit. Gritting my teeth, I focused.

In an explosion that rocked the cavern, the statue burst apart the black stone, flinging out wide enough that a few pieces even landed at my feet. I scooped one up and tucked it into a pocket, not really knowing why, but trusting my instinct. Perhaps I would need it later. Fiametta's back was to me, but I couldn't help but stare. "Mother goddess."

"Run, Dirt Girl. You won't get a second chance." Peta urged me forward, butting her head against the back of my legs. I stumbled forward, around the close corner and into Brand's home. I jogged to my room, stopping only to grab a cloth from the bathing room. Dipping it into a basin of water, I scrubbed at my face and arms. The mixture that flowed off me was a deep black, like coal dust. "There is no way—"

"Just hurry," Peta looked over her shoulder. "They are coming faster now. She already suspects you."

Great. I threw the wet cloth into the basin and bolted down the hall to my room. Peta slipped in as I shut the door. I stripped out of my vest and pants, dropping them onto the floor and then crawled into the bed. The silk sheets were cool on my skin and they covered the dirt on my legs, sticking to me where I was still wet. Peta curled up in the crook of my neck. "Until she commands you, do not open your eyes," she said as I closed my eyes just as the door to my room slammed open.

Even with Peta's warning, it was a struggle to lay relaxed, breathing slowly with my eyes closed tight.

"Terraling, awake," Fiametta commanded and I slowly opened my eyes. Blinking up at her, it was no effort to yawn.

"What's going on?" I whispered, sitting up and clutching the sheet to my chest.

Fiametta's eyes narrowed as she took a step closer. Once more I thought for just a split second I saw a glimmer of pink at the edges of her eyes. But it was gone before I could say for sure.

"How is it that your skin is damp?" Her words snapped me out of my musing.

I frowned and then gave a slow shrug, thinking fast. "Sweating, I guess. It is far hotter here than I'm used to at the Rim."

I didn't think her eyes could narrow more, but I was wrong. Her eyebrows dipped as her two Enders slipped into the room. I held up my hands, allowing the sheet to drop, baring my chest. "I am unarmed."

"I doubt that, as I doubt very much that you have been here all night. How did you keep awake when the bell tolled?" she said quietly, the tone of her voice anything but soft. Worm shit and green sticks, if she didn't believe me, there was nothing I could say to sway her.

Peta leapt to the floor, stretching. "My queen, the Dirt Girl has been here all night and I have slept beside her. What you are suggesting would imply that she has some sort of strength against our magic."

Fiametta's eyes flicked between Peta and me. She bent and scooped the cat up and I stiffened, feeling like she was touching something of mine that I hadn't given her permission to.

The queen held Peta up to her face. "And why should I believe you, bad luck cat?"

"Because my heart is here in the Pit, no matter where I am assigned by the mother goddess." There was a deep sincerity in her words and for some strange reason a slice of pain cut through me.

Fiametta sniffed. "We shall see." She lowered Peta to the ground gently. "Terraling, come with us. It is time for you to see your friend for the last time."

I grabbed at the sheets to keep from leaping out of the bed and showing all the dirt on my legs. "You said three days, today is only the second day."

An arch of her eyebrow and the Enders shifted on their feet. "And if I chose to kill him now, I would be within my rights."

I swallowed hard. "Is that what you've decided?" What would I do if she said yes? Try and raze the Pit? Take Ash out by force?

I would start a war between our families, a war the world could not afford; even I knew that much.

"No."

That one word and I deflated. "Thank the mother goddess."

"Do not thank her yet." Fiametta's words bit at me.

"Neither of you are safe. You may not be in the dungeon, you may have tried to save me from treachery, but I do not trust you. Nor will I. I feel you trying to worm your way into my good graces."

I couldn't stop my eyes from widening as she spun and strode out of my room. Her Enders followed silently. I rolled out of bed and jerked my still warm clothes back on.

What had Fiametta meant by that? Worming my way into her good graces, how was I supposed to be doing that?

Peta meowed at me and patted my knee with one paw. "Pick me up, Dirt Girl."

I bent and did as she asked and she curled onto my shoulder with a sigh that was one part relief and two parts pain.

My feet stopped in the threshold of my room, shock rolling through me as I sensed the pain deep in Peta's ribs. "Peta, did she hurt you?"

"It is her way with familiars, to get them to be honest." Her breathing was ragged and under my hands, several of her ribs felt lumpy, and out of place. The rage that lit along my nerve endings was sudden and sharp. That was the slice of pain I'd felt when Fiametta had picked up Peta. I strode out the door and through the house, fueled by anger.

Fiametta stood waiting with her arms crossed and I didn't slow. I all but slammed my face into hers, using my body to push her back. "If you touch my familiar again—ever—I will pull this mountain down on your head. Do you understand?"

Peta let out a whimper and hid her face behind my neck, but I never took my eyes from Fiametta. The two Enders swept in as I spoke, but she lifted a hand, stopping them. Her eyes were carefully neutral.

"She is a creature of the Pit and therefore mine to rule."

I pushed her back another step with my body, staring

down at her. "She is a creation of the mother goddess gifted to me. She is mine, Fiametta. Do not forget that."

Around us the mountain rumbled and the red lines of power worked up Fiametta's arms to her shoulders. "You wish to fight me, Terraling? You will lose."

"Do not be so sure," I snapped, seeing for the first time the colors racing up my own arms. A deep vibrant green with hints of pink peeking through, boosting the darker color. "You may be queen, but you are blind. You have someone trying to take you down and you are so sure of yourself, you think you can stand against it on your own."

Her blue eyes widened. "I have killed the traitor."

I took a step back and shook my head. "You think he worked alone? He said he had a master other than you. And then there are the firewyrms. You would wipe them out as if they were nothing."

"What do you know of the firewyrms?" She leaned toward me.

"I know they were being manipulated into attacking you. Making you believe they were the true threat."

Her eyes turned thoughtful. She raised her left hand and beckoned to the Ender on that side. "What say you?"

He bowed his head. "No one here rivals you, my queen. You reign supreme and will for a thousand years."

A second wave of her hand and both Enders stepped back, far enough that they could no longer overhear us.

The Ender's words had a feeling of something he'd said before; something he did by rote with no real feeling behind them.

Fiametta snorted. "That," she pointed at her Ender, "is why I have not killed you, Larkspur. You do not back down from me and while you irritate my skin just looking at you . . .I cannot deny you speak your mind and with it a truth I have not heard in a long time. It is an interesting theory you have regarding the firewyrms. Interesting indeed."

She lifted a hand toward Peta and I shifted my weight so the shoulder my cat sat on was away from Fiametta. The queen dropped her hand. "Come, see your friend. We will speak after of things that should not be heard by mere Enders."

Spinning on her booted heel, she walked away. Her long red hair swayed against the black leathers she wore as she walked . . . but the boots caught my attention.

Following slowly, I reached up and ran my hands carefully over Peta's back. "Why is the queen wearing boots? Why would she be afraid of her feet touching the ground or the heat? Shouldn't that be part of her connection to her element?"

I could understand why the Enders wore boots, they were useful when kicking the crap out of someone, but not the queen.

Peta gave a low shudder and she struggled to breathe around her words. "That is a good question."

I stopped and stared at her. "How badly are you hurt?"

"I will heal." Her eyes were at half-mast and her third eyelid dropped across her green irises. She struggled for breath as her tiny pink tongue hung out, and she wobbled on my shoulder.

"Fiametta, we must stop at the healer's first."

The queen never slowed for a beat. "I will not. You have a few moments before everyone in my kingdom will waken. This is your last chance to see your friend."

Peta panted in my ear. "She will not give you another opportunity."

Growling to myself, I stalked after Fiametta, wishing I could break a few of her ribs and see how she liked it.

Peta laid her head on my shoulder and a pitiful purr rolled

out of her, a raspy wet rumble that did not sound right. Jaw tight, I did my best not to jar or jostle her. Because maybe she wasn't all that enamored with being my familiar, but she was mine to protect and care for as much as I was hers.

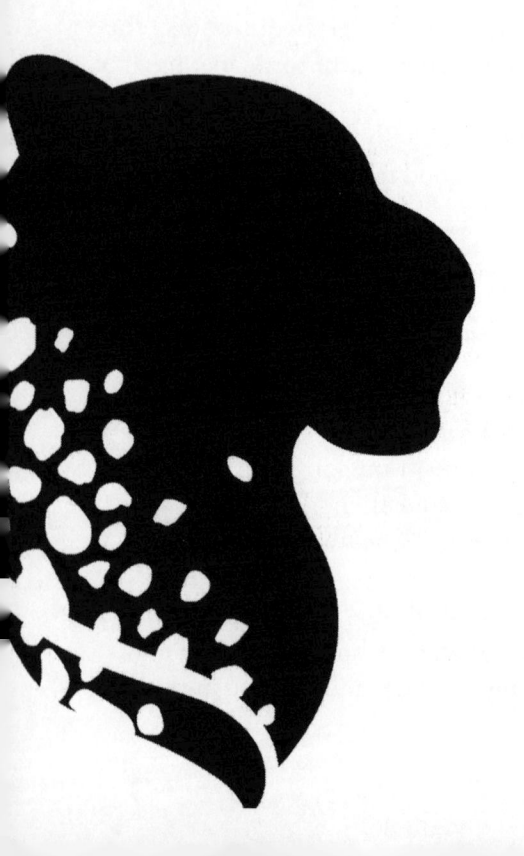

Chapter 14

The dungeons were not deep in the mountain as I expected, but to the side of the main throne room on the upper levels. The entrance was directly behind the gold and jewel encrusted throne.

Before I could ask, Fiametta pointed at the plain doors. "It is best to keep your enemies close, Terraling. If you ever find yourself protecting a royal in the Rim, that is advice I suggest you heed."

"Is that why you slept with the traitor?" The words popped out before I could catch them and I swallowed hard. Peta let out a low groan as the queen slowly turned.

Her blue eyes sparkled, and shocked, I realized she tried not to laugh. Her lips twitched and her shoulders tightened as she fought not to shake. Flicking her fingers at the two Enders, she turned and walked to the flat section of the wall that was the prison entrance. "Larkspur, you are bold like no one I have met in a long time. It is refreshing. I did not know he was a traitor. But if I had, I likely would have still bedded him. He had a very fine body."

I opened my mouth, but then closed it quickly as I thought better of my words. Fiametta turned and lifted an eyebrow.

"What, now you would censor yourself?" she asked.

"I believe if I cross a line you do not like, and I cannot see, you will use that as a reason to throw me into the dungeon beside Ash." I folded my arms over my chest while I waited for her to either open the door or step out of my way.

She shrugged. "Possibly, yes."

"Don't do it, Dirt Girl," Peta said at the same time as I spoke.

"And Cassava? Did you know what she was doing or did you realize too late that she was trying to manipulate you?"

Fiametta stared at me, her expression unreadable. "Cassava and I were friends once. Her machinations are what made me break ties with her. Basileus should have banished her when she killed his mistress. That one could have made your family great if she could have ousted Cassava."

Her words shocked me to the core. Fiametta spoke about my mother, Ulani. But Fiametta didn't know I was the bastard child of the king and I wanted to keep it that way. Swallowing the words I truly wanted to say, I kept it simple, my tone casual.

"So I hear." I didn't move from where I was. Anything I did now could be considered a threat. Fiametta walked toward me, circling me, her boot heels clicking against the smooth floor.

"What else do you hear? Tell me the truth, Larkspur, and

perhaps we can discuss your—and your friend's—usefulness to me."

She was behind me and I struggled not to turn to her. I did not want the queen at my back and my shoulder blades itched as though she'd pressed a knife there. I chose my words carefully while still speaking the truth.

"Cassava had a way of controlling people—it is why the king banished her."

Fiametta snorted as she came around my right side. "Your king has been under her spell for years. You think he's broken free because she is gone?"

Here it was, the stab in the dark. "Her ability to control people is gone."

Her eyebrows shot up and she stopped in front of me. "Truly?"

I nodded. "At least, her ability outside of her natural charms."

"Interesting." She turned and walked toward the dungeon again. "Come, see your friend before I kill him."

"Wait, you said—"

"You told me nothing I didn't already know. Cassava came to me first after she was banished. I sent her away with ease which told me she could no longer manipulate me as she once had."

She flung the doors open and gestured. "You have five minutes. If you are not out in that time frame, I will shut the door and lock you in."

I strode through, not for a second doubting her words. "Peta, count for me. Give me a ten second warning."

"Done," she said softly.

The gloom of the dungeon hung like steam in the air, moist and hot. The poor air quality not only made it hard to breathe, but hard to see.

"Ash?"

"Lark." His voice came from my left and I followed it unerringly. He was chained to the wall, his hands above his head and his legs spread wide. They'd stripped him down to nothing more than his small clothes. I stopped a couple feet from him.

"Are you hurt?"

"I've healed."

"Who did you fight with?"

He shook his head. "I don't even know. He was all dressed in black and I couldn't get a good look at him. I assumed he was another prisoner. He attacked me, and I fought back. I don't think he was expecting that."

The cloaked one. "He is no prisoner. He's fighting everything I'm doing to get you out."

"You can't get me out, Lark. They have a steel trap of a case. Brand should have had you out of here by now."

I leaned in and smacked him in the chest. "I'm not leaving without you. We're a team, we survived the Deep together, and we will damn well survive this."

A breath eased out of him. "There is nothing you can do, Lark. They have to blame someone for the deaths."

"Except that the Enders didn't die because of the wounds inflicted. They died afterward, something, or someone else killed them, Ash. I had paperwork that proved it—"

"Let me guess, the paperwork is missing?"

My whole body seemed to freeze despite the heat and humidity. "Yes, but how could you know that?"

"That is the way cases like this go. The minute you have hope it is snatched away and dashed. Let it go, Lark. I am here, willingly. The more you try to get me out, the more trouble you will find. We both know that."

He shook his head and I noticed his hair was dull with grime already, dimming the bright blond strands. He dropped his eyes and I felt his words like grease along my soul.

"No, that isn't going to fly, Ash. Stop lying to me. You don't really believe that."

His head snapped up and his mouth dropped which only confirmed the feeling. "How can you even know that?"

"Because she carries Spirit, you dumb dirt boy," Peta snapped and she carefully adjusted herself on my shoulders. "She's as loyal as they come and I would think you should be grateful someone is trying to free you."

His lips tightened and he shook his head. "Lark, this is goodbye. You can't save me and I . . . I want you to stop trying. This is my penance for losing your mother and Bram. They died on my watch."

I put my hands on my hips and glared at him. "Really? This bullshit again? Yes, they died. Yes, you should have stopped Cassava and her Sylphs from doing what they did." Peta sucked in a sharp breath that made her cough, but I kept going. "But the reality is you were as controlled as I was. As my father was—that is nothing we can change now or then. And now when I need you most, you would sacrifice your life for me which is all well and good, but what happens the next time?"

He frowned, "What do you mean the next time?"

Blowing out an exasperated sigh I threw my hands into the air. "You think this is the last time I'm going to be in trouble? It seems to be my middle name. The mother goddess has chosen me for something and I know I can't do it alone. Whatever it is. I have Peta now," I reached up and touched her head, "but I need you, too."

His golden eyes searched my face. "Lark."

"Ash, ask for a trial. It will slow things and give me time." I tipped my head to the side.

"You can't do that," Peta said, "he didn't ask for one in the beginning. He can't go back now."

Damn the Salamanders and their rules.

I started to back up. "I'm not giving up, Ash. "

The smile that flickered on his lips was all I needed. I stepped forward, cupped his face and kissed him. The heat between our mouths shot straight through me, warming me like nothing in the Pit had, not even the heat of the lava compared. I felt a need in him as our lips pressed against each other, as strong as there was a need in me to be assured we were together in this chaotic world. That even when everything else went to hell, we had each other.

I found myself clinging to him. No matter what happened, I couldn't lose him. I pulled back a little and rested my forehead against his as I caught my breath and my heart raced.

"For luck," I said.

"I doubt you will need luck," he whispered against my mouth.

Peta cleared her throat. "We must leave now."

I stepped back from Ash, spun and jogged out of the dungeon, trying not to think about that toe-curling kiss and the depth of emotion in it. I slipped through the doors as Fiametta's two Enders shut them.

But the queen was nowhere to be seen. I glanced around the room. "Looks like our conversation is done."

The Enders said nothing but I noticed they glared as they walked away. I couldn't resist. I lifted my hand and waved. "Say hello to Maggie for me."

The one on the left, the one who'd answered Fiametta's question stopped moving and his buddy smacked him on the arm. "Let it go. The queen will fry her ass before the week is out. You know that."

He grunted, put all four fingers to his neck and slid them across. "You're dead, Terraling. You will not see the start of the new moon."

I shrugged as if his words didn't bother me. "Fiametta is not the first ruler to threaten me. The funny thing is, I'm still here, and those who threatened me . . . not so much."

The Enders spun away and I stood, breathing hard. "You think they were telling the truth? Do you think Fiametta is playing me?"

"What do your instincts tell you?"

I drew in a slow breath as if tasting the air around us. "That nothing is as it seems here, any more than the Deep showed us its true colors until the very end. And that makes me nervous."

There was no way I could prove the Enders didn't die as a result of my weapons without the paperwork the cloaked one stole from me. No way I could show someone else ended their lives.

But how was I going to get Ash out? I paced the throne room, fatigue from the long night slowly creeping over me but I refused to give in. I had very little time to prove Ash was innocent.

Everything here in the Pit was about rules. . . that might be the answer I was looking for.

I stopped in the middle of the room. "The rules here are strict, Peta. And everyone follows them to the letter. Is there a place, like a library where I can look for maybe a loophole? Some way we can get Ash out?"

She shook her head hard enough that I thought she would fall off my shoulder. "No libraries here."

The lie was heavy between us and her eyes met mine. She blinked slowly several times. "I think we should go see your friend Cactus. He has some plants I'd like to taste."

It took me a good twenty seconds to realize she was afraid to talk here, so close to the queen's quarters.

So close to the place we'd be tossed and forgotten about if we stepped out of line.

"Fine, let's get you some greenery, you nutty cat."

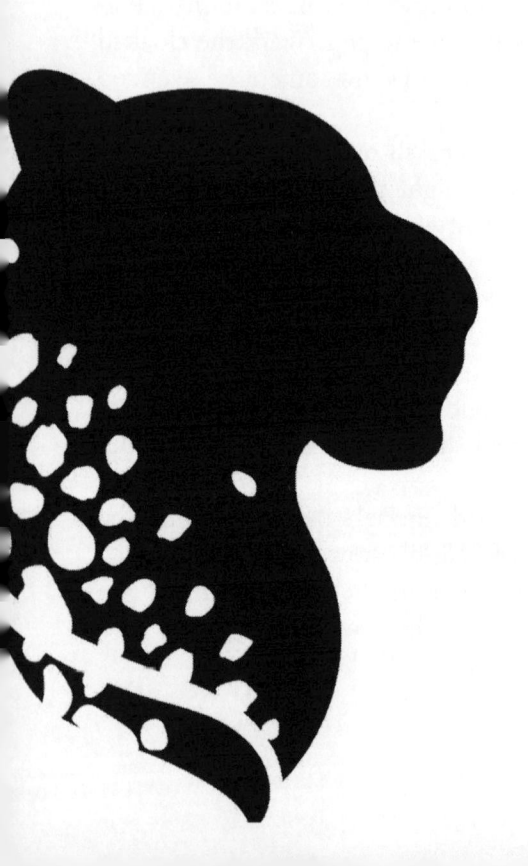

Chapter 15

Peta pointed out where I was to turn at each intersection and not once did we run into anyone. It took my sleep-deprived brain the whole walk to figure out something was not quite right. "How long before Fiametta wakes everyone else?"

"They should be awake by now," Peta said, "all the sconces are lit. I don't know why no one else is up. This has been happening more and more. Sleep is hanging onto people instead of leaving when it should."

Odd, but not necessarily bad. It meant I didn't have to explain to anyone what I was doing without a guide deep within the tunnels. Even with Peta on my shoulder I had no doubt I'd be stopped and dragged to the queen.

Again.

I stumbled over my own feet, my limbs dragging with fatigue. Peta gave a soft chirping noise. "We're almost there."

A few more steps, one last corner and we were in the main living area cavern. Daylight streamed through the light tubes and I guessed we were on our way to mid-morning. But still no one walked about, no children laughing and playing, no women doing laundry or cleaning.

A shiver ran down the length of my spine and I stopped and stared across the cavern. The only noise was of the bubbling lava river as it flowed in its winding curve.

I forced myself into a jog, my long legs eating up the distance between the bridge and us. While I didn't want to jostle Peta, I also didn't want to dawdle. Around us I felt the air tensing, like the very breath in the caves was being held; waiting for something inevitable to happen.

I really didn't want to find out what that event was going to be. Unfortunately for me, I was not to be so lucky.

When standing in the middle of the bridge, the structure groaned and Peta gasped. I didn't wait to see what the hell was going on but leapt for all I was worth for the far side.

Underneath me the bridge exploded, stones smashing into me as I flew through the air. Arms outstretched, the heat of the lava licked along the front of my body as I sailed toward land. We hit the edge of the river with a hard thump and I scrambled up the slight incline while the rocks dropped into the lava behind me, splashing and sending out droplets of red death.

Whatever fatigue I had was gone as I sprinted from the lava flow, my ears ringing with what had almost been the end of me. And no one would have known. Cactus and Ash would think I'd just abandoned them.

I finally stopped when Peta bit my ear and growled. "Dirt Girl, you're running the wrong way."

Breathing hard, I realized just how terrified I was—the very thought of falling into the lava drove logic from my mind. "I would face the Deep and its monsters a hundred times again before this," I spit out. The urge to keep running, to bolt until I found a way out of this nightmare labyrinth was overwhelming and I struggled to tamp it down.

"Dirt Girl, you will not go into the lava. I will not allow that to happen." Peta's words slowed my racing heart and I nodded.

Only then was I able to take in the scene. Exploding rocks and no warning—only one conclusion could be drawn. "That was no accident."

"I did not think so either. But who other than yourself can manipulate stone?"

"The smaller cloaked one." I stared around the cavern, looking for a black figure darting away, but saw nothing. That didn't mean I was wrong though.

"Cactus is capable. You must also think of him," Peta said and I hated that she was right.

He was a powerhouse in his own right. He'd broken the archway with such ease to stop the traitor from escaping.

"He could be helping her, and using our old ties to draw close to me."

I didn't have to say Fiametta's name. We both knew whom I meant. Peta bobbed her head. "True, but even though I suggested him, he doesn't seem the type. Do you truly believe you can't trust him?"

Getting my legs going again, I tossed the thoughts around in my head. "I don't know, Peta. That's the problem. Those who have been closest to me have shown they are rarely what they appear."

Peta cleared her tiny throat and whispered into my ear.

"My first charge, the one who carried Spirit was able to see inside other people's minds when he touched them. Perhaps you could do that with Cactus so you could be sure of his loyalty?"

I sucked in a slow breath. I'd done something similar when I'd been in the Deep. Though it had been an accident, I'd touched a shape shifter's head and heard his thoughts and what he planned on doing to me.

We were outside Cactus's home and I stopped in the doorway. I was totally stalling because I didn't know what to do, where to take this. I didn't want to believe Cactus could hurt me, and even as I thought it, the doubts faded. Yet I couldn't rule him out.

Carefully I took Peta from my shoulder and set her down. She limped through the door.

"You have a choice, depending on how much you trust the half breed."

She was right. I followed her into Cactus's home. The plants bent toward me and I brushed my face over the open hibiscus flowers, the soft petals a caress on my skin.

"How did it go with the queen?" Cactus broke the moment, startling me. I jumped, feeling as though my disloyal thoughts were written all over my face. I glanced at him.

"About as well as one could hope. Have you been here waiting the whole time?" I watched his eyes for a flicker, a sign of deception. He nodded and a half grin tipped his lips.

"Yeah, which sucks because Maggie is in the back snoring and farting up a storm. You know, Salamanders spend so much time in the lava that they begin to produce a kind of noxious sulfur of their own?" As he spoke he closed the distance between us, putting his arms around my waist and his chin on my shoulder. He drew in a slow, deep breath.

"And what do I smell like?"

His laugh rumbled across his chest to me. "Spring in the Rim, a little slice of heaven in my arms." He turned his head and I stepped back so his lips missed my neck.

"I need to speak to Peta, do you have another room away from Maggie?" I asked, folding my arms over my chest.

His eyebrows climbed. "Don't tell me you think Maggie and me—"

"You do whatever you want, prick," Peta snapped. "I need to speak with my charge alone."

Cactus laughed softly. "Maybe you will make her a good familiar, bad luck cat. At least you're loyal."

Peta gave a long low hiss and the fur along her spine stood at attention. I bent and scooped her up even though she'd just asked to be put down. "A room, Cactus."

He gestured to the left and a doorway I hadn't noticed before opened. "Lark, you know me. Maggie isn't my type in the least."

I nodded, feeling a weight around my heart lift. "I know, Cactus. Still, it looked bad." Stopping in the doorway, I looked at him and placed a hand on his chest when he would follow me. "Peta, this is your call."

Her body trembled, but I didn't look down at her. The seconds ticked by, almost audibly as we waited for her answer. A sigh slipped out of her. "If you trust him, then I will too. He may hear what I have to say."

And even though I'd doubted for a moment, I did trust Cactus. He was my friend.

Cactus grinned and I turned my back on him, entering the smaller room. I struggled not to gasp at what I saw.

Four tiny redwoods were planted in the hard ground; they couldn't have been more than a few years old as they barely reached the ceiling. Without a second though, I reached out and touched one, my hand aching for the feel of home after so much time in the Deep, and now, trapped in the Pit.

This is what Banishment would be like. To always be aching for a place that speaks to your soul, yet never able to hold it in your hands or heart again. The thought came unbidden to my mind and I closed my eyes against the sudden blur of tears.

Banishment was what every elemental feared, that they would be cast out of their home, doomed to wander the world until they faded to nothing, their souls and very beings starved of the connections that made them who they were. "Cactus, how is it you've survived this long outside the Rim?" I whispered as I pressed my head against the tree. Its soul was young, and very old at the same time. The history of its species called to me from the long distant past, the wisdom they held in their collective memory if I could just understand the words whispered around me.

"The fire is a part of me too, Lark. As long as I have some of the earth near me like this, I can do it. But . . . I can't stay here any longer. There is more of me that is of the earth than fire."

I opened my eyes to see him mimicking me, his hands and forehead pressed against the tree to my right.

Peta let out a small sigh. "Then we must all escape. And soon. I feel a firestorm coming, and none of us will want to be here for that."

Her words brought me back to the moment, breaking the spell the trees cast over me, calling me home.

"Where do we go first, Peta? You know the Pit, where do I go for answers?"

She shifted her weight and dropped her head to my ear. "There is a secret place that Loam would go. A place only a few knew about and they are all dead and gone now. A place of old rules that even the queen can't deny."

A shiver ran through my spine. I looked to Cactus. "Do you know what she's talking about?"

He frowned. "Whispers of rumors. Stories of a place that tells our history and everything that has ever happened in the elemental world. That would be a huge library though and even here, hard to hide."

Peta shook her head a single time. "No, this place is very small. It is where all the original edicts of the Pit were created. Loam knew about it. He had to as an ambassador. And of course, the queen knows, but she doesn't know *where* it is."

"But Loam did?" I needed to be very certain because if Peta was wrong, I knew there was only one thing I could do to save Ash. Something he would fight me on every step of the way, so I held it as a last resort. A final gamble if I found no other way.

Forcing my feet to move, I stepped away from the trees and out of the room. "Peta, take us there."

"Now?" Her strangled squawk was all I needed to hear to know just how dangerous this was going to be.

"Yes. Now."

Chapter 16

As we walked, I held Peta in my arms. I felt the struggle of her body with each breath she took, her broken ribs at a bad angle pressed against her lungs.

"That's why I can't shift right now," she said softly. "A shift when I'm so injured would surely puncture my air bags and I would be of no use."

I stroked a hand along her back as I followed Cactus through the currently well-lit tunnels. Empty tunnels.

"Cactus, stop a minute." I laid my hand on Peta's back, and spoke quietly to her. "We're connected, aren't we?"

Her green eyes narrowed. "We are."

"And I can draw energy from you, if I need to be healed?"

She slowly nodded. "Yes."

I closed my eyes. "Then let's reverse the flow." I found the bundle of emotions, the connection to Peta inside my head, right next to the place that my power with Spirit resided. Distantly I heard her saying it didn't work that way, that I couldn't heal her but I couldn't see why not. It made sense that it—the connection between us—would work both ways.

Taking hold of my Spirit power and the bond to Peta I threaded them together inside my head. The strands around Peta's energy glowed a bright pink, like a sun flare, and then faded into nothing. Peta let out a gasp and I swayed where I stood.

A dip in my energy was all I felt, but when I opened my eyes Peta glared up at me. "Stupid Dirt Girl! You aren't supposed to sacrifice your life for me, it's supposed to be the other way around!"

I shrugged and she leapt from my arms, immediately shifting to her snow leopard form.

Her emotions were all over the map, swinging from an intense dislike that came from years of being told Terralings were stupid and useless, to an intense loyalty that bordered on love.

Confusion I understood. So I gave her an out. A way to not feel like she was being a burden. "I can't have you slowing us down," I said, brushing off my shirt.

Her back stiffened. "I would not have slowed you down."

I looked to Cactus who gave me a wink as he patted her at the base of her tail, the equivalent of an ass pat on a woman. "Yeah, you were, kitten."

"Kitten?" She spluttered the word and I moved between them before he could make it worse. The last thing I needed was her lashing out at him. Even if he did kinda deserve it.

"Peta, just lead the way, please. I'll talk to Cactus."

Her long tail sliced through the air, side to side, actually hitting the wall, but she did as I asked.

Cactus settled in beside me and he opened his mouth but I beat him to it.

"Why is no one else awake yet?"

His eyes widened. "Shit."

"Yeah, that's what I'm thinking."

Peta glanced back at us. "This isn't the first time it's happened. Eighty years ago, the queen's father kept everyone in a subdued sleep while he hunted a threat to the throne."

My mouth dropped open. "That's what Fiametta's doing. I told her there was more than one threat, that her lover Coal was answering to someone."

Cactus stopped at the next intersection. "I have to go to her then."

"What, why?" I stopped with him and Peta turned.

"I'm one of her enforcers, Lark. Not an Ender. I'm just brought out as a threat. She may be a hard ass, but she is still my queen. She needs to be protected." He leaned in to kiss me and I turned my face so he only caught my cheek with his lips.

"You aren't making any sense. Cactus, if she sees you're awake when she put you to sleep with everyone else, what do you think she's going to say? Thanks for waking up on your own to protect me?"

Peta snorted. "More like, 'Ah, so here is my traitor. I'll just kill him and be done with it. No one will miss him.'"

Cactus paled. "Shit."

"You keep saying that."

Peta brushed against my thigh, her fur warm under my hand. I threaded my fingers through her long fur.

"Cactus, we can't wait. Either you're with me, or you want to risk the queen's suspicion that you're one of the traitors."

His jaw was tight, but he nodded. "Damn, there is no choice for me, is there?"

Peta shook her head. "No, there isn't. As is often the way with life."

There was no more discussion after that. Peta trotted in front of us and we jogged to keep up. She wove her way through the maze of hallways until she reached a dead end. A fountain of bubbling water stood in front of us, steam rising from the tiny pool. The fountain itself was made of hardened lava and shaped like a snarling tiger. The water poured out of the tiger's mouth into the pond it stood in.

"The water is boiled as it comes through the tiger," Peta said.

"Should have it pour out its ass," I muttered. My only experience with a tiger was one that Maggie sent after me. So maybe I was more than a little prejudiced against that particular big cat.

Peta sniffed. "Yes, that would be fitting for a tiger, blowing smoke out its asshole."

Cactus burst out laughing and then slapped his hand over his mouth as he winked. "Sorry." Obviously not that sorry.

Ignoring him, I approached the fountain. "Peta, this is a dead end."

"No, it's not." She dipped her face until her whiskers touched the boiling water. "You must reach in to find the thing to press. I don't know what it is, Loam never told me. But he would reach in here, and something would click and then the wall behind us would open."

Her eyes lifted to mine. "This is why I'm angry you healed me, Dirt Girl. You need your strength for this."

Cactus stepped forward. "I'll do it. I can hold the heat at bay a little."

Peta shook her head. "No, you can't. That is what

everyone thinks but the heat is a part of the water. Only a water elemental could truly pass this without injury."

"That doesn't make sense," I said. "Why would you want an Undine to be the only one to escape injury?"

Peta shrugged. "I didn't make the rules."

I put a hand on Cactus's arm. "I'll try first, if I can't find the latch, you can try."

His jaw ticked but he didn't argue. We all knew our time was limited at best; no, that wasn't true. Ash's time was what was running out.

Taking a deep breath, I wiggled the fingers on my left hand. No point in damaging my dominant hand if I didn't have to. "How deep, Peta?"

"To your elbow at least, based on what I saw Loam do."

"Shit," I whispered. "Cactus, stand by the wall. When the door opens, hold it if you have to," then before I could stall any longer, I plunged my hand and forearm into the water.

The sensation was just like that of being tested by the mother goddess. My skin scorched instantly and I whimpered as I forced more of my hand in until I felt the slight bump of something under my hand. I jammed it hard and yanked my arm out. But the boiling water had done its damage. My hand and arm were bright red, and tiny boils broke out. I held my arm out from my body and waved it in the air, which only made the blood pulse stronger.

"Draw on me, Dirt Girl. Loam did, I know the pain will be temporary," Peta said.

Gritting my teeth, I nodded. The pain was excruciating, and I knew now why the pool was set up that only an Undine could pass it easily. They didn't like coming to the Pit in the first place so the likelihood of them finding this hidden place was small. But more than that, there was no way I could hide the injury from the queen. I had no doubt that was the reason behind the boiling water. How could you hide where you'd been?

The simple answer was—you couldn't.

Peta's energy flowed through me and I drank it down, like a bucket of ice water poured over my skin, as though her heritage in the mountains flowed through her veins into mine. The burn faded and I let go of Peta's energy as soon as the pain was tolerable.

Peta pushed herself against me. "Fiametta will know, you should take more from me."

"I'll wear a long shirt," I said. "I can't take all your strength, Peta. I need you. And I don't like causing you pain. How often did Loam come here?"

"Daily." Her green eyes glittered with what I thought might have been tears, but she looked away before I could be sure.

"Ladies," Cactus said and we both turned. He stood in a doorway that hadn't been there only moments before.

Peta and I jogged forward and slipped through the door into the semi darkness. Cactus let go of the edge of the door and the panel behind us slid shut. A bloom of fire lit over Cactus's hand. He moved forward and lit torches ensconced in the walls. The tiny place lit up as though we had noonday sun beating down on our heads. Bright shiny reflective panels covered the ceiling, picking up light and throwing it around with abandon.

The walls were lined with books and scrolls and the place felt . . .old. Not that it was dusty, in fact it was remarkably clean. Twenty by twenty feet across, it was by no means a large room. But there was history here, like it was the first place the mountain had given up to be used by an elemental. The age of the place seemed to settle in my lungs as I breathed, the feel of the past becoming a part of my body.

I walked to the far side of the room and put a hand on

the spine of the first book that stood out. "The Divining of Souls," I said and dropped my hand. "Not quite what we're looking for."

Peta nosed the books near her. "These are about controlling lava at the highest level."

We skimmed the books, looking for something that would lead in the right direction. I froze in front of a thick book with pale leather so light, it could almost be called pink. The color isn't what stopped me though, but the title etched into the spine as though with a rough tipped knife.

Destroying Spirit Elementals.

I pulled the book from the shelf and held it in my hand. *Distant cries of terror, the beating of hearts slowing, the breath of a final goodbye to those they loved.*

With a hard shove I jammed it back onto the shelf. Ash's life was on the line, I needed to keep focused on that. I could always come back for the other book.

That's what I told myself anyway.

"I think there is something here," Cactus said, his excitement contagious. Peta and I ran to him and he held out a book at least twelve inches thick, and easily as wide. He flopped it onto the floor and opened it. The pages were so thin that the words on either side bled through and made the words difficult to read.

"Are you sure?" I frowned. A not so small part of me hoped the answers were not in it. The thing was monstrous and I doubted anyone had bothered with a table of contents, or goddess forbid, an index of some sort.

Cactus held the book up so I could read the cover. "Elemental Law." Damn it, that was not what I wanted to see with the time we had left.

I sat beside him and started to thumb through the pages. "Look for key words like Ender or execution."

We sat like that through most of the day, ignoring our

stomachs' demands for food or drink, ignoring the fatigue that finally caught up to me. We were halfway through the book when a bell sounded. A bell that could only mean one thing.

"The day is over," Peta said softly, yawning. "I'm sorry, Dirt Girl, your friend will die in the morning."

I skimmed the page I was on, the words blurring, but they were all I had left to stop the execution. This was the other option I'd sought, the fail safe that would allow me to stave off Ash's execution.

Unable to fight the combination of the sleep spell and my own lack of sleep, I lay on the hard floor next to Peta. Cactus curled up behind me, his body a vibrant heat that soothed my aching muscles.

I clung to the two of them, knowing what I had to do when the morning came, and knowing they both would be furious with me.

But as far as I was concerned, it was the only way to save Ash, and it would buy us the time we needed.

At least, I hoped it would.

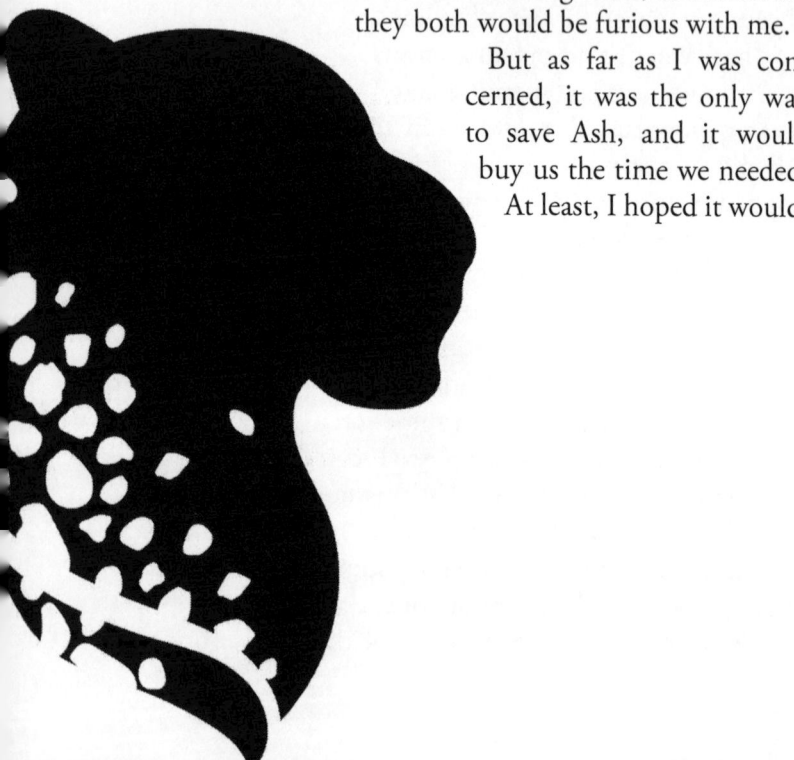

Chapter 17

I dreamed of fire and lava spilling over me as I screamed out my last breath, Peta's eyes glowed as she laughed, and I sank under a wave of red death. Scar's eyes glittered as Maggie tore him apart. "Save me," he called out.

Jerking awake, I sat straight up, my heart pounding and my body covered in a fine sheet of sweat that evaporated as I slowed my breathing.

Beside me, Peta in her snow leopard form purred in her sleep, obviously her dreams were not anything like mine. Then again, she wasn't planning what I was. Cactus lay flat on his back with his hands linked over his belly, a soft smile on his face.

I pushed myself to my feet and went back to the big book of Elemental Law. That last page was still there, the words as solid as they'd been the previous night. Carefully, I tore the page out, folding it and tucking it inside my vest. Turning back to my two companions, I clapped my hands together.

"Come on, you two, time to wake up."

Peta yawned and stretched, sticking her butt in the air as she arched her back toward the ground. "The dawn is coming, we have to hurry if you want to say goodbye to your friend."

I nodded, but kept my thoughts to myself. The last thing I needed was Peta or Cactus trying to stop me. We woke Cactus and the three of us left the tiny library. The tiger fountain continued to bubble and boil, and I knew I would not be able to help if they had to go back into the library. "Cactus, can you get messages out of the Pit?"

"Probably, why?"

This was the key to my plan, if we were to all get out of the Pit alive. "I need you to contact Belladonna. Tell her we need her help as an ambassador. Can you do that right now?"

He nodded. "I don't think she'll get here before the execution, Lark. Not even if she Travels."

"Just go, and hurry," I said.

His green eyes held more than a bit of suspicion as if he wondered what I was really up to. I knew because I would wonder the same thing if our roles were reversed. "Trust me, Cactus."

"I do." This time his kiss landed square on my lips and I kissed him back. In case I was wrong and what I was about to do would cost me my life. Which was a distinct possibility.

For a split second, he held my face. "Don't do anything stupid, Lark."

"Would I do that?"

"To save someone you love, yes. You would." Still, he let me go and I watched him as he turned at the next intersection and was gone before I could say anything else.

"He knows me too well."

"What are you doing, Dirt Girl?"

Now that he was gone, I decided to tell Peta, since she was stuck with me and the choice I made. "I'm going to confess."

"No!" she roared and put herself in front of me, halting my moving forward, her snow leopard form big enough to physically stop me. "I will not allow it. You and I both know those Enders were killed after they were healing. You would at most have a lashing, and yet even that would kill you here in the Pit! Your death is not deserved, Larkspur. You can't do this." Her voice trembled and I dropped to my knees, wrapping my arms around her thick furry neck. She pressed her mouth against my collarbone, her teeth flat against my skin chattering with her emotions. Through our bond her intention was clear. To stop me no matter what it took. I hadn't really expected her to be so firm in her conviction.

"Peta, I don't plan to die. Belladonna will get me out of this and if I have to . . . I will fight my way out."

She gasped against my neck and I pulled back. "I'm not like the other elementals. I won't go down without a fight. Trust me. Please."

"You would be banished, anathema to all who met you. Your life would be over; you would be the walking dead. For what? A single life freely given in exchange for yours?" Her mouth hung open on the last word as if she couldn't believe the words even as she said them.

"No one will die, Peta." The words sounded hollow in my own ears, and seemed to bounce off the walls followed by a low laugh, as though the words themselves mocked me.

I put my hand on her. "Peta." Just her name, and she dropped her head.

Her green eyes rolled up so she could look at me. "Larkspur, please do not ask me to do this. To watch you offer up your life. You will be the thirteenth charge the mother goddess has given me. I cannot bear to watch you die, too."

"Walk with me." I put my hip against her shoulder and she gave way. We were close enough to the throne room that even if she refused to point out the turns, I could have found my way. The large doors beckoned and behind them I heard the rumble of voices, in particular Fiametta's husky tone.

"Trust me to come out of this alive, Peta."

"That is what my first Spirit charge said right before he died trying to save a friend," she whispered and I wasn't sure I was supposed to hear her.

I was committed though. Ash would not die.

I put my hands on the door and pushed against the sparkling firewyrm etched into the solid gold. They swung open with ease and when I stepped into the throne room, all activity stopped and every eye looked to me.

Ash was on his knees in front of Fiametta, his head bowed. Fiametta was dressed in her black Ender leathers and her hair was wild around her face, like a living flame, moving on unseen winds.

"Terraling, I thought you were going to miss your friend's final walk," she said as she smiled at me.

I smiled back, though it was an effort and my lips felt as if they were numb from ice. "I doubt that. Fiametta, I confess to the deaths of the four Enders and take all the consequences that will come my way as a result of this confession." I crossed my arms and waited for a beat before I continued. "I instructed this Ender to confess in my place."

Fiametta's eyebrows climbed. "Truly? And why would he do that? You are the younger of the two, obviously less experienced as an Ender. Why would he listen to you?"

I drew myself up to my full height and arched an eyebrow right back at her. "Because I am a princess of the Rim, and he is marked as my bodyguard."

The entire room sucked in a sharp breath, including Peta at my side.

Ash let out a low groan. "No, Lark, do not do this."

Fiametta stalked slowly toward me, though her voice was even and without emotion. "You think you can avoid punishment because you have royal blood? If anything, you are held to a higher standard."

"Do you accept my confession and release Ash?"

Fiametta laughed. "No, I will not. You are a smart girl, Terraling. Very smart. You would take his place, then ask for a trial and try to find a way not to be thrown into the Pit, yes?"

I held my breath and kept my mouth shut, but still, she saw through me. Damn, maybe Belladonna wouldn't be able to help. Fighting my way out was not something I wanted to do, but I *would* if I had to.

Nodding she smiled again. There wasn't a drop of condescension in her. "You will not take his place, though I commend you for trying to save your friend. Very admirable."

From under my vest I pulled the one sheet I'd taken from the book of Elemental Law. The thin sheet fluttered in the heat wafting through the room. I read it out loud. "It is my right as a royal of the Rim to take his place and his punishment in his stead. By law."

Fiametta reached out and carefully took the paper from me. Her blue eyes darted as she skimmed the page. "Where did you get this?"

"It does not matter. This is law, regardless what family I would stand in."

Fiametta lifted one hand and the lines of red flowed up her arms as she called on her element. Before she could burn the paper, I snatched it away.

Her eyes bugged out and the struggle on her face was momentary. "Come with me. Now. The rest of you wait here."

She spun on her heel and I followed her out of sheer curiosity if nothing else. Why hadn't she just allowed us to switch places?

Fiametta led me to her personal chamber, and when Peta moved as if to follow me in, the queen stopped her. "This is not for you, familiar. I see your hand in this; you took her to the library, giving her access that only Loam had." She pointed at the paper I still clutched.

Peta tipped her head to one side. "You are not my queen any longer, Fiametta. I obey Larkspur, no one else."

Fiametta's hands clutched at her side, the only indicator that Peta's words affected her at all.

I put a hand on Peta's head. "Wait for me. Please."

Peta nodded and sat on her haunches. "I will come if you call."

Fiametta swept into her room and again, I followed. The door slammed behind me seemingly of its own volition.

"You are going to get us all killed, you idiot," the queen snapped at me, all pretenses apparently dropped.

"Actually, I'm doing my best to get my people out of here."

Her eyes narrowed. "Do you not wonder why there are so few Salamanders awake? Has it not crossed your mind that perhaps your friend's life is a miniscule drop in the scheme of things?"

How in the goddess's name was I supposed to know any of that? "Why did you bring me here?"

She began to pace, her power zipping along her arms and over her body as her agitation increased. "There are at least two more traitors within my home, Terraling. You found one, I want you to find these other two. If I have you in chains, I can hardly use you to ferret them out. And if you don't manage that . . . those threatening me and my people have made it very clear they will wipe us all out. You and your friends included."

This was not what I expected but I would use it to my advantage.

"And if I do? Will you let Ash go?"

"No."

I burst out laughing; I couldn't help it. "That doesn't make me want to help you at all. If Ash will die either way, what does it matter to me if *you* survive your traitors?"

Pausing by the bed, she stroked the sheet with one hand and flames licked along it, but didn't burn it. "The traitor has been leaving me notes, breaking into my room and taunting me while I sleep."

A shiver ran through me. "As bad as that is, it has nothing to do with me."

"That's what you think." Her eyes lifted to mine. "His words lead me to believe you are also a target seeing as he is encouraging me to wipe out the three Terralings in the Pit. You, Ash, and my Cactus."

I swallowed hard. "Charge me with the deaths of the Enders, and allow me to go on trial. That gives me a reason to be in the Pit longer."

"No."

Anger sliced through what was left of my reason and I took hold of the power of the earth running through me. I softened the ground under her feet and sunk her to her neck in a split second. She gasped and stared up at me. "You would dare attack me?"

I crouched in front of her. "I am not attacking you, Fiametta. I am stopping you from doing something foolish. If I must, I will fight my way out of the Pit. Do you understand? I will pull this wyrm-ridden mountain down on your head. I will keep those who are mine safe, no matter the cost."

Standing, my heart beat with fear as much as anger. I knew I was playing a dangerous game. "Do you think the traitor will leave you alive if I don't let you go and he finds you imprisoned like this tonight?"

"My Enders will—"

"They will do nothing when they see a proclamation of release written on your paper." I walked to her desk and opened the drawer, pulling out a thick piece of parchment. "Will they?"

"Terraling—"

"My name is Larkspur." I corrected her as I laid down the paper and picked up the pen.

"I will hunt you to the ends of the world."

"Not if one of the traitors kills you first. Which I'm banking on." I scratched a few words on the paper as Fiametta struggled. With her arms pinned to her sides, it would take her time to blast her way out.

"I will . . . negotiate." She bit the words out and I turned to see her eyes blazing and the lines of power running along the tops of her shoulders. She was fighting to get out and failing.

I swallowed hard and realized the anger had fled me and I couldn't connect to the earth. "Worm shit."

"Let me out, Terra—Larkspur. We will negotiate when I am free." She tipped her head back as if she could look down her nose at me while imprisoned.

"Peta," I called out, and she burst through the door a second later. Lowering her body to the floor, she crept toward Fiametta.

"Lark, what . . ." she stood and looked at me. "What has happened?"

"I need you to get Cactus. Hurry." Peta gave a quick nod and bounded away without another question.

Fiametta struggled against my bonds and I felt them

crack, lava pushing through the rock I'd ensconced her body in. "Terraling, if one of my people sees me like this I will kill you."

I dropped to a crouch in front of her, feeling the heat through the earth as she tried to power through the rock. I had to have a reason to call Cactus, or she would see my weakness. "Fia, can I call you Fia? There is a problem. I don't trust you to keep to your word." I patted her on top of the head and for just a moment I thought she might snap her teeth at me.

A breath went out of her. "You are . . . not what I would expect from a princess of the Rim. Or an Ender from the Rim. Or really anyone from the Rim."

"Why? Because Cassava told you we were weak?"

Fiametta laughed, and I had to hand it to her. She handled things like a queen. Calm, cool, and reasonable. To a degree. Not to say I trusted her by any stretch of the imagination.

"That. And I have seen your father deal with people. Even Cassava who he should have killed, yet only banished."

I swallowed hard. "Yes, I agree."

Fiametta nodded at me. "Who is the heir to the Rim?"

Shrugging, I looked over my shoulder to the door, hoping Peta could find Cactus quickly. "I don't know."

Fiametta leaned her head back. "You are powerful enough to be the heir, yet you are not a full Terraling. You don't have the look. So that would make you a half breed. Like Cactus."

"Yes."

"What is your other half?"

I clamped my mouth shut and shook my head.

Fiametta's eyes narrowed and she stared hard at me. "No fire runs in your veins, no water either. Perhaps Sylph? You have the height for a wind walker, but not the temperament."

"I favor my father's side," I said softly.

Her eyes didn't waver and for just a second I met them. I didn't want her to guess my other half, didn't want her to know I could manipulate Spirit. And it hit me in that moment I could have forced her to agree with me.

"You've thought of something, Larkspur."

The door behind us creaked open and I twisted on my feet. Cactus stepped into the room, followed by Peta and . . . Brand.

Brand's eyes widened and he pulled a crossbow from his back, had the bolt set and aimed at me before I could even stand. "Terraling, you go too far."

I slowly held my hands up. "She and I are negotiating. As two royals houses do from time to time."

Fiametta snorted. "Shoot her, Brand."

His finger hovered over the trigger and I tensed. "If I move when you shoot, you will hit your queen."

Brand wavered, his bow dipping. "My queen, she is correct."

"I just need witnesses to this negotiation," I said. "The queen is letting Ash go. In return, I will search out the remaining traitors within the Pit."

Peta cleared her throat. "And then we will leave without pursuit. Make sure you add that in."

I glanced at the big cat. "Yes, there will be no punishment or pursuit regardless of how I find the traitors. Regardless of who I may have to injure or even kill to do as you ask."

Fiametta growled under her breath. "Fine. Let it be done."

I stood and rubbed my hands together. "Bring her out, Cactus."

Cactus gave a start. "Me? You put her in there, you pull her out."

Glaring at him, I pointed at Fiametta. "Pull her out, or I'll leave you behind when I go."

"Damn, you're cranky when you haven't had breakfast." He dropped to his knees and pressed his hands into the stone, softening the rock around Fiametta. Brand rushed forward and helped his queen out of the stone. She whispered something to him and he spun, the crossbow flying toward my head.

I ducked, but the bow still hit me, slamming into my shoulder. I stumbled backward and went for my spear as Peta leapt in front of me. A ring of fire burst up around us, like a cage that increasingly shrank.

Fiametta stood over me. "These two men are loyal to me, you didn't really think any negotiation we made in front of them would hold, did you?"

Pinned to the ground, Peta laid her body over mine, protecting me from the heat, I stared up at Fiametta. "You know, I'm beginning to think the rulers of all the families are assholes."

The door swung open with a bang behind us but I couldn't see who it was. However, the voice, when I heard it, made me want to weep with relief.

"That's my sister you have unlawfully restrained."

Belladonna
had arrived.

Chapter 18

Things moved quickly after that and not in the direction I'd been hoping for. Manacles were clamped onto my wrists and I was dragged to the dungeon along with Peta and Ash. The steam filled, gloomy rooms were almost a relief to the constant dry heat of the rest of the Pit.

Strung up by my wrists, Ash was on my left and Peta was chained in her leopard form by the neck on the right. I leaned against the wall behind me. "I'm beginning to think this is our thing."

Ash gave a low grunt. "What do you mean, our thing?"

I tugged at the chains, knowing they were more than just metal and actually blocked our ability to reach our power, not unlike our own cells at home did. "This is the third dungeon we've been in together. Think we can make it four for four?"

He rolled his head toward me. "Are you trying to be funny while we're locked up waiting to be pushed into a bubbling pool of lava?"

I shrugged. "Maybe. You aren't laughing, so I'm guessing—"

"Lark, stop it. We aren't going to survive this. I thought I could at least get you out of here and now you've gone and screwed that up."

"What?" I couldn't believe what I was hearing. "Are you serious?"

"One thing, I asked one thing of you—to go with Brand and save your own life—and you couldn't even do that."

The disappointment in his voice cut through me like a knife, reminding me of just how many times I'd disappointed my father and those around me. I turned my head away, letting my hair fall forward to hide the tears that fell. Peta gave a soft cry and tried to reach me but we were too far apart.

"Larkspur . . . are you . . . crying?" The sound of chains rattling and the shuffling of his feet filled the space around us. I kept my head turned away, it shouldn't hurt so much, but there had been a part of me that so badly wanted to prove to Ash that I could do this on my own. That I could get him out of here; that I could get us all out of here.

My pride had sunk that particular ship.

"Lark, I was trying to make you angry. I don't really mean what I said," Ash said. "I thought that was what you were asking of me, when you started talking about being in here together."

I wiped my cheeks as best I could with the side of my arm and turned to him but got no further than opening my mouth.

The main doors clanged open and in swept Belladonna, her pale red and yellow skirts swirling in the steam. She came to a stop in front of us, her hands clasped behind her back. "Larkspur, I see you're in trouble again."

I managed a smile, but even I knew it was weak at best. "Yeah, looks like I could use some help."

"I can get you out on a technicality, but not Ash." She raised a hand, stopping me from interrupting. "We won't leave him, I promise. But for now, let me get you out of here. It may be all I can do before I leave."

"Leave, what's going on?" My first thought was of home, of the Rim and all that could have happened in the short time since I'd been gone. Bella shook her head.

"I am the interim ruler of the Rim. Father has gone . . .away for a time."

I jerked at my chains. "Away. What do you mean?"

She shook her head. "Now is not the time. We can discuss it when you are home. But I must go back swiftly, things are unsettled there. Our siblings are causing problems. Of all, can you believe Keeda is being the worst?"

I could. Our younger sister was a great deal like their mother, Cassava.

I nodded and she snapped her fingers. Brand came forward out of the gloom and unlocked my manacles and Peta's. He didn't apologize for swinging his crossbow at me, and I didn't apologize for sinking Fiametta into the ground. His movements were jerky and more than once he banged the manacles against my wrists as he removed them.

"Bella," I said, "what was the technicality?"

"You are still assigned to me as a bodyguard. And since I am here, I need you at my side." She smiled, though there was a distant pain in her eyes. "I'm glad you called for my help, because I could not have come unless you asked for it. As per my instructions."

"You . . . you wanted to come on your own?" We walked out of the dungeon and into the throne room where Fiametta waited. She didn't have a chance to answer me.

Bella's whole demeanor changed, from the way she walked to the tilt of her head. Regal was the first thought that hit the front of my brain. Of course, none of that mattered in the moments that followed.

Fiametta smiled. "Lark, I will take your confession now. You will be tried for the death of the four Enders, and Ash's life will be held in trust as if it were your own."

"Shit," Bella whispered under her breath and I had to agree. This was what I wanted, but if I understood Fiametta correctly, Ash would still be killed if I were found guilty.

Belladonna stepped forward. "No trial is needed."

"What?" Shock flickered through me like lightning through a summer sky—a sharp flash followed by the certainty I hadn't seen what I'd thought I'd seen. Or in this case, heard.

My sister held her hand out to Fiametta and those few around us—mostly Enders and one old man who held a pen over a piece of parchment—fell silent. "There does not need to be a trial. It is a waste of time. The law states for an Ender to kill another Ender is death."

Fiametta nodded, her eyes narrowing ever so slightly. "This is true."

Belladonna smiled. "Larkspur has confessed to killing four of your Enders. You accept this as truth?"

I made a choking sound and Bella glared at me. "Be quiet, I'm about to save you."

The queen's eyes narrowed farther. "I do accept that as truth." What the hell was my sister up to? She was making my sentence of death a certainty.

She snapped her fingers at the old man and he scuttled forward. I didn't recognize him but he was a Terraling by his deep brown eyes and tanned skin. "My lady." He bowed as he held out the parchment. Bella took it and handed it to Fiametta.

"Would you read it out loud please?" Bella asked, her voice dripping with sweetness. "I ask only because another person might be accused of lying, and speaking only what they wish to be heard. As the queen, you will be above such reproach. Just read the outlined section please."

Fiametta snapped the paper and then began to read. "If any Ender should kill another Ender, they shall be sentenced to death. As Enders are trained to the highest skill level with weapons and magic they shall be held to a higher standard." Fiametta blew out a breath. "This is nothing new, Belladonna."

"Please, the next few lines are the most important." She clasped her hands together, holding them at her waist.

Fiametta shrugged. "But should an Ender be killed by someone not with that title, their death shall be considered just. If those trained to the highest standard fall, it is to be their time to return to the mother goddess."

Bella held her hand out to Fiametta, taking the paper back. "This is truth?"

"Yes, of course it is," Fiametta snapped and then her eyes widened. The net Belladonna had carefully laid seemed to visibly settle over her. "Damn, you are your mother's daughter. Clever girl."

"In this case, I will thank you, and take that as a compliment." Belladonna lifted one hand, palm upward. "Your Enders were killed before Larkspur took her final testing to *become* an Ender in full. Therefore she is within her rights, and they were meant to return to the mother goddess. You may not execute her, or Ash in her stead."

Bella swept toward me, but Fiametta stopped her. "Belladonna, read the next line on that paper . . . *if* you will."

My sister closed her eyes and I knew that whatever happened next on the sheet was going to be bad. Her hand trembled so I took the paper from her, unfolding it so I could read the remainder of the section.

The words were about as shitty as I could have imagined. "Those who kill an Ender shall yet be punished, for death is not to be taken lightly. And the one who shall mete out that punishment will be the ruler of the house the Enders were taken from." I lowered the paper and looked straight at Fiametta. "I assume you have something in mind?"

Her smile was not nice, the edges of her lips hard with cruelty. "I have just the thing for a spoiled royal who thinks she can come into my home and do whatever she pleases without facing a single consequence." She walked up to me and leaned in close, her words only for my ears. "A royal who will not willingly help another ruler." She clapped her hands together and Brand strode forward, handing her a coil of rope.

Fiametta pointed the coil at me—leather, not rope—"Strip her."

Belladonna gasped. "You can't truly mean to do to this."

"Cassava has obviously misled you, little Terraling. We are not friends, and neither are our families." Fiametta uncoiled the rope and her hands lit up as she called on the fire. Like a living snake it wrapped around the leather, lighting it.

My sister spun to me. "Lark, fight her!"

Peta trembled beside me, her fear bleeding into my heart. "Lark, this is not a punishment you can survive, the lava whip is deadly to any who don't carry fire in their veins."

Fiametta shrugged. "You won't do as I ask. Unless you have changed your mind?"

All I had to do was agree to help her hunt the traitors, the two that on my own I would have gone after.

Pride had gotten me into this mess. Perhaps humility would allow me to find a way out. "I will do . . . as you ask."

There was a heavy pause in the air and she patted me on the head. "Well done. I will only give you half the lashes." She smirked and my jaw dropped.

Maggie stepped forward. "How I have waited for this. Better even than the Pit, your death will be slow." Along with two other Enders she grabbed me and they stripped the clothes from my body, leaving me as bare as the day I was born.

"On your knees," Fiametta commanded and I dropped, a slow steady fury building in my guts. How could she do this in front of her people, and they allow it? The answer was simple. The same way the people of the Deep had bowed to Requiem. The same way my own family had bowed to Cassava.

Child, do not fight her. This is part of your training, this is part of your journey. Hold tightly to the earth, hold tightly to me and I will see you through this. The mother goddess spoke softly and I reached for the power underneath my knees. The mountain's essence filled me, like a cup overflowing with water and I squeezed it, wrapping it around me.

The whip sailed through the air, cracking at the last second before it touched my back. At first I thought I would be spared the pain as the lash left my back, for a split second I felt nothing.

I was so very wrong.

A blaze of pain roared up my spine, tracing the lines of the whip as if a serpent made of pure fire had lain across my skin. I couldn't stop the cry that escaped and I heard it echoed from Bella, as she sobbed. Echoed in Peta as she cried out with me.

The lash fell again and I collapsed to my hands and knees, the pain cutting through me, feeling as though it would truly divide my body wherever it touched. I lost count how many times the whip burned over my body, time receded and I floated in a place where my body and spirit seemed to have disconnected from my mind.

In that haze, an intense hatred blossomed. Fiametta, and Requiem. Leaders of two families of elementals and neither deserved the position, nor the power. Yet they were given it. Even my own father was a complete mess, his mind and spirit twisted by Cassava to the point he was unable to trust past the fear. The mother goddess had allowed it to happen, and had allowed this to happen.

I was the one being punished for deaths I hadn't caused.

The world was not fair. I knew that and was not fool enough to think otherwise. But this was too far. The anger powered through me and I clung to it, riding it like a wild horse that would carry me into battle. The whip was coming, the sound of it in the air cut through every other noise around me. I pushed myself up so I was on my knees.

Looking over my shoulder at Fiametta as she wielded the whip, I saw something I didn't expect. Her face was a mask of sorrow, and even . . . grief. As if she didn't want to hurt me.

"Enough, you'll kill her!" a voice cut through the pain, and the whip didn't make contact with me, but fell to the ground, twisting and writhing with the flame that licked along its length.

Cactus stepped between me and Fiametta, his hands in front of him, lines of power running up his arms in green and red; he was ready to fight for me against his own queen and the thought stunned me. I could count on one hand the number of people who'd stood for me in my life, placing my life above theirs.

My body burned, every breath I drew into my lungs

stretched the skin over my back and I wished I didn't have to breathe at all. Yet I stayed where I was, swaying, but upright.

Fiametta's blue eyes held mine. "The punishment is done."

The anger didn't leave me, but my strength finally did and I slid to the floor, flat on my belly.

My cheek pressed into the cold stone below me and a shiver coursed through me, which cracked open the burns on my back, the crispy skin cracking. Belladonna dropped beside me, her hands on my face.

I didn't know what she said, the words blurred by the waves of pain rippling through me, wiping out anything that made sense. I closed my eyes and held tightly to the only thing I knew would get me through.

Rage.

Chapter 19

Cactus knelt beside me, his words breaking through the buzzing in my ears. "You can't Travel with her like this. She has to heal first." His hands were gentle, touching me only where the lash hadn't fallen. My face, front of my neck and palms were the only safe zones I could feel.

Peta pushed him away and dropped her face to mine. "Lark, draw from me."

I knew the pain would transfer to her, and I wasn't willing to do that. I couldn't manage much more than the one word.

"No."

She let out a soft cry and lowered herself to the ground beside me, but spoke over her shoulder. "I will carry her."

Hands lifted me, cracking the skin on my back yet

again, the warm blood oozing down my sides and into Peta's fur as they laid me on her back, still face down. In my head, I knew she couldn't possibly move smoother than a stretcher held by two people, yet I didn't feel her steps. She dropped into a stalking crouch and crept forward, her paws barely rising from the ground. I rolled in and out of consciousness, my nerve endings driving the pain deeper into my body. I couldn't stop the twitching of my muscles as I fought the agony that wanted to break me. In that moment, I understood that was the full purpose of the lashing—not just to wound me, or kill me, but ultimately break my spirit—to bring me to my knees and make me pliable to Fiametta's will.

"Bring her in."

I lifted my eyes. We were back at Brand's home, and Smoke directed Peta to take me to my room.

"No, not here."

Peta gave a low growl. "You have no choice. The healers are still sleeping." I doubted that. More likely that Fiametta refused to allow them to help me. For just a moment my anger overwhelmed the pain, giving me a brief second of relief.

The relief evaporated like my sweat as Cactus tucked his hands under my shoulders and Brand took hold of my feet.

As careful as they were when they moved me from Peta's back to the bed, I couldn't stop the sharp cry from my lips. I blacked out, the fiery pain driving straight through my consciousness, cutting me off from the world in a fogged haze.

A soft hand on my brow brought me around and I turned my head, pressing my cheek into the silken sheet below me. "Smoke."

"Shh. You must rest. I have something for your back. It will draw the heat out but . . . it will be very painful."

I tried to turn so I could see her face but she pressed her hand against my head. "Lark, you must not move. You will be scarred as it is, but every time you move, you make it worse."

My entire view consisted of: the pale blue sheets, Peta's green eyes as she sat in her housecat form beside me with her tail wrapped around my neck, and the grey stone of the far wall. I kept my breathing shallow and my voice low. "Do it, Smoke. If it means I will heal faster, then do it."

"The wrap will take an hour to prepare. Rest and whatever you do, don't move," she said and walked away, her footsteps fading. The sounds of the household were dim, humming in my ears with the drone of a beehive. Peta stiffened. "Lark, he's coming."

"Who?" I mumbled the question, the pain causing a weird drowsy state I couldn't seem to fight. Peta's head dropped forward and she let out a long, low hiss as her eyes closed.

Footsteps, the sound of the door opening and then the flash of a black cloak along the edges of my vision. "Dear Larkspur, that bitch really did a number on you, didn't she?"

He dropped into a crouch so he could look me in the eye, except that his cloak hid his facial features from me. I knew nothing except he was a man, and part of the reason I had the lashing. If he hadn't taken the papers from me I could have made a case that the Enders were not fatally injured. That they'd been wounded, but that was all.

The pain made my tongue loosen. "What did you do to my cat?"

"She's sleeping, like everyone else here. You know, the Salamanders are a foolishly proud group. They think they are safe here in their little mountain. But I'll tell you a secret.

. . they aren't. They have enemies. The firewyrms hate them with a passion."

"You made them enemies, didn't you?"

He gave me a wink. "Maybe I did help it along a little."

"And you are making the Salamanders sleep."

Laughing, he nodded. "Yes, it makes the queen twitchy. And of course, I was the one who finished off the Enders. You must have guessed that by now."

I blinked several times, unable to nod.

He laughed and leaned forward. "I like you, Larkspur. I always have. I wish I could trust you." With one hand, he reached out and touched my nose. On his middle finger was a deep red chunk of ruby set into a silver band. Lines of power flickered around it as though it were alive. It could only be one thing: the elemental stone that controlled fire.

"Nice ring, your momma give it to you?" I slurred.

"As a matter of fact, she did. Quite the woman my mother was." He withdrew his hand and tipped his head to one side. "You'll be leaving after this little fiasco?"

I tried to think what the point would be in lying to him. Why would I stay now? Fiametta proclaimed Ash and I could leave, and Cactus and Peta were free to go as well, as far as I knew. I vaguely recalled Belladonna saying goodbye. That the Rim needed her. No reason to say, and yet, I wanted to cover my ass in case something slowed me.

"Unless someone forces my hand, yes, I'll be leaving as soon as I heal," I murmured.

"Ah, lovely, just lovely. You'll leave Fiametta to me then. I like that. Sorry about the bridge earlier. I was under the impression you were helping Fia—by the way, love the nickname you gave her—to straighten things out here. Can't have that, now can I?"

My tongue was thick and all I wanted was a drink. A long, cold drink. "Water."

"Oh, of course. Here." He held out his hand, and in his palm, water pooled, clear as a river coursing from the top of a mountain. He held his hand to my mouth and another time I would have hesitated, questioned his seeming kindness. But the fire in me burned hot, devouring the moisture in my body at a rate I didn't think I could keep up. He tipped his hand and the water trickled into my mouth at a steady rate until I turned my face away. "Enough."

He stood, took one step away and then stopped. "May I make a suggestion, Larkspur?"

I stared up at him, wondering if he really was asking. The whole conversation felt like he'd just wanted to talk. Which was weird at best. "Only if you tell me your name."

"Ah, yes, everyone wants to know my name. You can call me Blackbird. On account of the black cloak."

Internally, I struggled with what to do. He was an Undine, wearing a ring that gave him power of a Salamander. How the hell was I supposed to stop him? And did I even want to?

"Did I meet you when I was in the Deep?" I spit the question out as I tried to place him. He shook his head.

"We've met, Larkspur, and I like you. But you will never, ever guess who I am." He slapped his hand onto my back, his fingers burying into my soft, tender flesh, blood oozing out. My back arched and I screamed as he dug his fingers deeper into the wound.

"I'm doing this for your own good. You'll thank me later. And if you care to blame anyone, blame the mother goddess. She asked me to heal you and that is the only reason I do what I do for you. I am sworn to her."

At least that was what I thought he said; I struggled to

hear anything over my own howls into the air. His hand seemed to sink through what was left of the flesh on my back and to my bones, his fingers sliding along my spine.

I couldn't even lash out at him. My body convulsed with pain to the point of being stunned. A rolling, crushing wave that stole my ability to breathe, think, or even consider anything beyond my next heartbeat and wondering if it would stop and the pain would end.

As suddenly as it began, he took his hand away, bent and put his lips next to my ear. "I'm sorry your back is not pristine as it was. I cannot heal what is no longer there, and Fiametta didn't leave me much to work with." He pressed his cheek against mine. "Leave tomorrow, Larkspur. Or I will make you wish Fiametta had her lava whip again."

He kissed me on the cheek and with a swirl of his cloak was gone.

I sat up and took a few steps after him before I realized what I was doing. Freezing in place I lifted my arms. My left arm had been burned badly, but now there was no pain.

Behind me, Peta yowled and leapt to the floor, her tiny feet sounding more like she was in her leopard form. "Lark, your back, it's healed. How can that be? What happened?"

Wobbling as I turned, I shook my head. "The one in the cloak, he did it."

"The one who tried to drop the bridge out from under you? That makes no sense."

I put a hand to my head. "No, it doesn't."

Weak, exhausted from the lashing and subsequent healing, I lay back down on the bed. "Peta, get Cactus and Ash. Tell them we leave as soon as I wake."

She nodded and I closed my eyes so I might have imagined the rough-tongued lick across my forehead.

I sunk into a sleep so deep, I knew it was not just fatigue, or pain induced. No, this was something more.

I'd felt her touch before, and knew it well.

The mother goddess wanted to speak to me. Which was just as well since I had a few questions for her.

Chapter 20

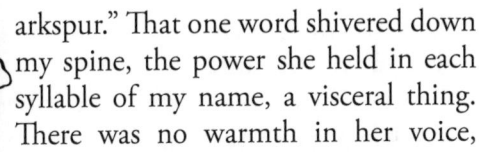

"Larkspur." That one word shivered down my spine, the power she held in each syllable of my name, a visceral thing. There was no warmth in her voice, not like before. She called to me and I was forced to answer.

Blinking, I sat up. We were in the Rim, the towering redwoods swaying lightly in the breeze. Low hanging clouds flowed through the boughs of cedar, but unlike the normal white, they spread in pale purple filaments that seemed to cling to everything. The mother goddess stood next to the biggest redwood in the forest, the sides of it easily reaching fifteen feet to either side of her. The dark red color of the trunk offset the soft cream dress the mother goddess wore, her long pale gold hair a shade lighter than mine. A part of me was disturbed that she always chose to come to me in the guise of my own, long dead mother.

I bowed my head. "Mother."

"Child, you have saved Ash from death. Well done." Her hand touched the top of my head.

Questions bubbled up on my tongue and I struggled to figure out where to start.

"Just say the words as they come, Larkspur." She spoke quietly, but with authority and I stopped trying to think too much about what I had to say.

"The man in the cloak, he calls himself Blackbird. Why would you tell him to heal me? He's an asshole." Okay, maybe that was a bit too bold for conversing with a goddess, but I had to know. I lifted my head a fraction of an inch so I could look up at her.

Her eyes were closed as if deep in thought.

"He is my child, as are you. He serves me in his own way, though you will not understand his part in your life until your journey is close to an end. The balance must be kept. For everything good, there is something vile." There was a heavy pause as she drew in a deep breath. "And now I will ask of you one more thing, a task I know you will fight. A task you perhaps have already guessed."

Shivers of fear trickled through me. Her words were enough to set me on edge and send my mind into a whirling maelstrom of questions. "I am your servant," I whispered.

"You will stay in the Pit and save the firewyrms."

"Why don't you just stop Fiametta? What could I possibly do that would be better than you showing up and putting her in her place?"

Her lips quirked upward at the edges and she crouched beside me, her knees tightly together as she leaned over them toward me. "Child, there are rules that define this world, rules even for one such as myself. My consort flaunts the rules as he tries to influence things," she reached out and touched the griffin tooth hanging from my neck, "and one day he will suffer for it. Remember this, if you remember nothing else. The rules set in place are to protect you, to keep you safe and your soul intact."

I couldn't stop the sigh that slipped out. "So long story short, you mean you can't stop Fiametta?"

"That is correct. Rules and free will, they are a juxtaposition that has existed from the beginning of time." She stood in a single smooth motion that made it seem as if she'd never been crouched beside me. "Save the firewyrms, Larkspur. That is what I want of you, and in doing so, you will save many lives."

The mother goddess put her hands on my back, a soft breath escaping her that sounded like a whisper of pain. "You should not have been punished, but I cannot turn back time. We all make mistakes, Larkspur. Even I have." Her fingers trailed the deep pits and ruts of the wounds and I could see the terrain as though I looked at a painting. My back was all but destroyed, muscles and ligaments burned apart, my spine peeking through in places, exposed to the open air. The man in the cloak, Blackbird, though I doubted that was his true name, may have healed me, but as he'd said, he could not put back what was no longer there.

Her fingers felt like a butterfly dancing across my skin. "Save the firewyrms, and I will make this right."

My jaw dropped and again anger curled upward like a creeping vine that no matter how you dug, you never truly got all the roots. They always found purchase somewhere else.

"Heal me first," I said, not dropping my eyes.

The mother goddess stared at me, her eyes emotionless, but her tone held more than a little anger. "This is not a negotiation, child."

"I believe it is. Who else have you got within the Pit with the strength to possibly stop Fiametta?" A small part of me struggled to understand why I was fighting her on this.

The mother goddess took a step back. "You are walking a fine line between obedience and outright defiance. That is not a line you can balance for long and you will have to decide if you are truly one of my children, or one of the banished."

The threat was clear. Do as she wanted or be cast out to die alone. I bowed my head, but said nothing.

Sleep rolled over me in a wave, dragging me down into the place of dreams and nightmares. The mother goddess was gone and I found myself on my knees again, reliving the fire whip as it seared through my back. I jerked awake and a hand rubbed through the back of my hair. "Easy, Lark. It's over."

Ash's voice soothed the fear and I lowered my head to the bed once more. One of his arms encircled my waist and he pulled me against him. The warmth radiating from his body into mine eased the aches and residual tension my muscles held.

I rolled in his arms and buried my face against his neck, breathing him in. A soft, furred body curled up at the back of my neck. Peta dropped her head into the crook of my neck. "Sleep, Lark. Sleep and in the morning we will leave."

But would I leave? Or would I do as the mother goddess commanded? My thoughts jumbled together; my body twitching and jerking as I fell into a fitful sleep. Disobeying her would mean I was leaving the firewyrms to fight on their own. Scar's eyes floated through my mind, the soft glimmer of amethyst.

The morning came soon enough, the light shimmering through the reflective tunnels above bringing me out of my stupor. Voices drifted to me, like dust motes floating in the air. Smoke's voice was the same husky pitch but pain laced her words.

"I don't care. Just . . .he can't be gone. He can't be. He was my baby." A sob rippled out of her and I was up and moving before I could think better of it. Ash was beside me and threw a sheet around my body, but not before he gasped.

"Lark, your back."

"I know it looks like worm tunnels and goose shit."

"No, it's not," Ash said, his hand on my arm stopping me. The arm he held was the one burned. But the burn was completely gone and in its place a tattoo rested on my skin. A vine of deepest green with thorns of a dark purple curled over my muscles.

"Your back is more of the same," he said.

The mother goddess had healed me after all. I closed my eyes and whispered my thanks to her.

Another cry from Smoke turned my attention back to the moment at hand.

I stumbled forward as my legs tried to buckle. How long was I out? I thought it was just a day, but the last time I'd felt like this, I'd been coming out of a week of trials with the mother goddess.

The main living area was lit with soft burning candles, their light flickering over the sober faces. Brand sat beside Smoke, holding her tightly as tears ran down his face. The two older boys, Stryker and his brother Cano stood against the far wall, their faces also wet with tears as their chests heaved.

Stryker stepped forward, "Mom, I didn't know; none of us did."

Brand stood as Smoke held a hand out to her oldest son, drawing him to her until she held him against her chest. "I know it's not your fault. The mother goddess has turned her eyes away from our people."

Her words shocked me and I had to bite down on the question that formed. Where was Tinder? The little boy with the sparkling eyes and the bright personality? The one with the questions that were never ending?

I gasped as the understanding hit me in the chest. The how of it didn't really matter, but I knew . . . Tinder was gone. Brand's eyes flicked to me, and there was no malice in them.

"You are free to go, Terralings. Fiametta has declared you are not to be stopped." He dropped his eyes and tightened his hold on his wife. I stepped forward and went to my knees beside Smoke. She'd been kind to me, one of the few in the Pit who had.

"Smoke."

Her eyes flicked to mine, the gray centers that so resembled her name were awash with tears. "It is not safe here for you, Lark."

I shook my head. "It looks as though it is not safe for you either. How did it happen?"

"I said," Brand grabbed my arm and hauled me up to my feet, "you are free to go. Isn't that enough?"

I didn't jerk away from him, but stepped into his guard. "Tell me what happened. Maybe I can help."

Ash let out a soft groan. "This is going to be the Deep all over again."

I cast a glare at Ash and he said nothing more. Brand tightened his grip on my arm, and for a moment the pressure reached the point where I thought I would have to back down as my tendons were squeezed over my forearm bones.

"We went to swim in the Pit," Stryker said, breaking the silence. Brand let go of me, his hand falling to his side. Stryker stepped forward and circled his arms around his mother, holding her as much as she was holding him. Stryker's young frame trembled from his jaw to his bobbing knee. "Tinder ran ahead of us and jumped into the Pit. He was fine, laughing and splashing. I swear it."

I frowned, but said nothing. Someone must have struck at Tinder, someone had to have hurt him. Yet I struggled to see someone hurting a child, especially one as likeable as he.

An image of Bram being stolen from my arms hit me like a runaway bull and I sucked in a quiet breath. Logically I knew Cassava had no reason to attack Tinder. Even if I did have a soft spot for the little boy, what did it gain her? Nothing was the simple answer, yet I couldn't help but want to blame her for another death. It took all I had to remain quiet and let Stryker speak when he was ready.

His eyes were distant as if he were seeing something only he could see. A shiver ran lightly through his body.

"I almost jumped in. I stopped at the edge and yelled down to him and he looked up at me, a funny expression on his face and then he just . . . the lava *burned* him like he wasn't a Salamander, so fast, like he was nothing and then he was sucked down and gone. Like he was never there. He didn't even have time to cry out, it was so fast. There were other kids, same thing happened. Seven or eight of them, just . . . gone." Stryker dropped his head as a sob rippled out of him.

Smoke stroked his hair with one hand, whispering a song to him, the words inaudible but the tune soothing, even to me.

I put a hand over my eyes, seeing all too easily little Tinder sucked down under a wave of lava. Saw his eyes full of pain and confusion, of all the years he could have had, stolen from him.

Like Bram.

"Take me to Fiametta," I said, not bothering to hide the thickness of my words, the way tears clogged my throat. I would stay, because I couldn't leave when children were being killed. Whatever I could do, I would.

"You can't do anything, Lark." Brand shook his head. "No one can."

I slowly straightened my spine to my full height, softening my words at the last moment. He'd lost his son, the least I could do was remember the pain of that loss. "Are you sure?"

We stared at each other, and maybe there would have been more said. But that chance would never come.

Footsteps pounded toward us, a staccato that didn't sound good. An Ender, young and new to the title by the looks of the acne on his face, stuck his head in the door. His words were gasped, out of breath as he was.

"The lava is flowing."

Brand snorted. "It always is."

The young Ender shook his head. "No, it's out of control."

Brand stood and strode toward him. "Fiametta will deal with—"

The kid shook his head again, harder and it was then I saw the fear stamped on his face. "No, that's just it. The lava is wild, and even the queen can't stop it."

A collective breath was drawn in and held within the room. I may not have been a Salamander, but even I knew news couldn't get much worse.

The funny thing about assumptions is when you are proven wrong, it's amazing just how very wrong you can be.

Chapter 21

Brand led the way, running out of the house, his hands going to his weapons. "All of you stay inside!"

I leapt after him ignoring the fact I was wearing nothing more than a silk sheet; there was no way I was going to sit inside and wait for a river of lava to roll over me. Outside their home, the steady growing noise I'd been hearing became clear. The lava flowed over the banks of the river, rushing with a speed that seemed to pick up even as I stared at it.

"Pigeon balls," I whispered to myself. The heat had at least tripled just in stepping outside of the walls. All my thoughts of staying and helping, of bringing Fiametta to justice for the deaths of the firewyrms was swept away with the reality of our situation. "We have to get out of here."

Ash put a hand on me. "We have to get to the Traveling room. That's our only way out."

I nodded and Peta butted her head against my leg. "Lark, look at the lava."

I did as she asked as an Ender stepped toward the flowing red death, letting it wrap around his legs as if it were water.

Except that it wasn't water; not even for him. He screamed as the lower half of his body sunk, dissolving as we watched. Someone gasped, it might have been Smoke, but it might have been me too. The Ender writhed and struggled as he slowly died, his upper body twitching as the lava slipped up over his waist, his head dropping so his chin rested on his chest and then his whole body lit on fire.

On fire.

His element no longer protecting him.

What in the mother goddess's name was going on?

You can save them all, Larkspur, if you are brave enough. Her voice whispered to me. I wanted to shake my head but a small part of me wanted to believe her.

I grabbed Brand by the arm. "We have to assume that could happen to any of you. We need to get to Fiametta."

The younger Ender, Jack by his hasty introduction, nodded. "That's the plan. The queen is going to deal with this but she wants all her people with her."

Brand herded his family after Jack. "Go with him. I want to see how deep this goes."

Smoke's eyes glistened. "Be careful, my love, I can't lose you, too."

He reached for her and they kissed, a mere brush of lip against lip and yet there was emotion enough that once more I felt I was witnessing something special, and intimate. I glanced away.

Ash touched my arm. "You need to get dressed."

Without a word, I strode toward the house and tried not to think about the way the Ender had fallen to the lava. As if he were nothing--as frail and mortal as any human. How could that be? Our elements didn't just leave us, they didn't stop working for no reason.

I had my pants on and was tightening the straps on my vest as the thoughts racing through my head slowed, and with them my hands.

Peta leapt on the bed and put her paws on my chest. "I sense it in you. What have you thought of?"

I stared at the wall as my mind settled on the realization like a bird landing softly on the spindly branch of a too small tree. The weight of it slid over my shoulders. "Someone is blocking their ability. Just like my ability was blocked by Cassava when I was young," I whispered the words. "It has to be the cloaked one. Blackbird."

"That's impossible," Peta said. "You saw it yourself. He is an Undine who also carries Spirit and he also can reach the earth. And he is carrying a ring tied to fire. That would mean . . . three elements isn't possible." Yet her voice wavered at the end.

Ash stuck his head in, breaking up our conversation. "We have to move if we're going to get to the Traveling room."

Following Ash, who in turn followed Brand, we made our way to the far side of the living quarters to a ladder cut into the mountain. Brand gestured. "You three get up there. Peta, you can lead them to the Traveling room from there."

She nodded, and leapt up several rungs to hang for a moment as she answered. "Hurry."

Ash held his hand out to Brand and the fire elemental slowly took it. "The lava is rising fast, and the Traveling room lies below it."

"Understood," Ash said, letting go. "Be safe my friend."

Brand turned away and I knew if he went, we wouldn't see him again. Smoke would lose yet another piece of her heart.

I called after him. "Brand."

He didn't stop.

"Brand, you will break her if you do this. She deserves better."

His whole body stiffened. The air in the cavern thickened with black smoke and I thought he wouldn't turn.

"Damn you, Terraling." He spun toward us and pulled himself up the ladder after Peta who scrambled ahead of him.

I climbed after him, Ash on my heels and I realized we were missing someone. "Cactus, where is he?"

"The queen asked for him while you were out," Ash answered and then there was no air for questions, barely air for breathing.

At the top of the ladder, the thick smoke hung dark enough to dim the glittering light that lit the tunnels. Brand didn't reach back for me, which was fine. I crawled over the lip of the ladder, coughing as I struggled to breathe. Ash wasn't doing any better and we scooted forward until the air cleared a little.

Brand led us toward the Traveling room, stopping at the stairwell that led down to it. I peered past him to stare at the bubbling lava that curled up the steps toward us. That made the decision easy. No going home that way.

He didn't pause though. "The queen has a backup pair of armbands in her chambers. She'll let you use those. I don't know where they will take you though."

"Unless she's using them to get her people out of here," Peta said softly, padding ahead of us at a steady trot. She seemed totally unperturbed by the events slowly piling up. Events that had no real meaning I could see other than to wipe out the Salamanders.

The facts seemed to be that someone was trying to kill them. And I was pretty sure I knew who. It was just a matter of whether or not I could stop him.

That was the real problem; how did I find the man who called himself Blackbird and kick his ass if he carried three elements within himself? Three elements he was strong enough in that he could easily take me out. Not to mention he also carried the ring that gave him power over fire.

Brand stopped suddenly and I almost walked into him, so deep within my own thoughts as I was.

The healer's room doors were flung wide and while there was a bustling trade going on, there was almost no noise. Fiametta strode from table to table, talking to those patients laid out. Her hands brushed against cheeks, touched skin that wasn't broken with heat blisters, gave comfort where she could.

Clearing his throat, Brand got her attention. "My queen, the Traveling room is cut off."

"I see." She walked toward us, her blue eyes cool. "I suppose you want the bands from my room."

Brand nodded. "I can get them myself."

"Do that." Her words were soft, like the precursor of rain as clouds were driven in on high, silent winds. I braced myself, facing her head on.

"You think we did this somehow."

Her eyes narrowed and I expected to see lines of power running up her arms, except there was nothing. "If I thought that, I would kill you myself right now. No, this is the work of the traitors. Which you have agreed to help me find. I suggest now that you are healed, you get on it."

Ash shifted beside me and I recognized the pose. He was prepping a move that would allow him to leap up and drive both fists directly into Fiametta's throat. Her eyes narrowed. Of course she would recognize it, being a former Ender. As much as I hated her for whipping me as she had, a part of me understood that it was the law. Even I couldn't deny it.

I put a hand on his arm. Our eyes met and he relaxed—a little, anyway.

"I know who did this," I said, just as Cactus stepped into the room. He had a long burn up his left arm and there was soot all over his face, which made his eyes stand out even more, but he was at least intact.

He gave me a wink and blew Ash a kiss. "Good to see you two made it out all right."

"Don't speak too soon, pet," Fiametta said and then turned to me once more. "What do you think has been done, Terraling?" Her voice dropped into almost a coo, that I recognized for what it was.

Dangerous.

This was the tricky part, yet there was no nice way to speak the truth. I fought not to cross my arms over my chest; I had done nothing, and yet I felt like I was already defending myself. "Your power has been blocked. And that's why your element has turned on you."

Someone from the table to the right of us moaned. "The mother goddess has turned her eyes from us. We have offended her and now she will cleanse her children of their sins."

Fiametta didn't move. "How could you know this if you were not the one—"

"Because Cassava has done it to me in the past. It is possible, and it's the only thing that makes sense. It is the power of Spirit being used on you." I waved my hand at the room, and the people in it. "How else would you explain this? Your people burning in their own element? Your inability to reach your power? The firewyrms attacking for no reason? Your inability to see reason . . . all of it can be attributed to someone manipulating Spirit. I just never would have thought it could be used on this scale."

The queen lifted her hand and there was a flicker of red

tracing the inner edge of her arm. She was trying to pull on her power, but the lines flickered and died like a flame being snuffed. Her shoulder's slumped. "Damn you for being right. This is why those who carry Spirit are killed on sight."

Her back straightened as fast as it had slumped. "Ender," she pointed at young Jack, "I want everyone out of the mountain. Immediately."

He clapped his hands together, and barked out orders. "You heard her, everyone head to the entrance, take nothing but the clothes on your back."

Smit, the healer who tended me several times, made eye contact with me. I jogged to his side and slid an arm around his patient, a young girl probably of an age with Stryker. "I can carry her."

He nodded. "She can help you find the entrance."

Peta shifted beside me. "I can take someone."

Smit snorted. "Bad luck cat, I don't think so."

I put a hand on him, tightening my fingers over his forearm. "Her name is Peta, and if you call her a bad luck cat again, I will forget you are a healer."

His eyes flicked between us. He swallowed hard. "I thought the rumor was wrong about her being your familiar. Pardon me."

Peta snorted and I shifted the young girl to her back. Smit handed me two small kids with burns on the soles of their feet. Their tiny whimpers shot through me, piercing me to the core. What was the point of this, hurting children, making them suffer for something as materialistic as a crown? What did Blackbird truly hope to gain? Was it just the crown, or was I missing something?

En masse, we left the healer's rooms, a long line of people that curled through the tunnels. In the distance was the sound of the ocean, only I knew it wasn't water washing against the inside of the mountain, but lava roaring out of control. Ash was just ahead of me also packing a young man, his feet burned, piggy backed style.

"Ash, can you block the lava behind us?"

He shook his head. "No, I can't reach my power either. Whatever is blocking the Salamanders isn't choosy; it's blocking every elemental."

And there was too much fear in me to reach my anger and thereby reach the power of the earth. The idea traced along my mind that maybe I could use Spirit on Ash and unblock his ability but I knew so little. What if I hurt him?

I had to trust we would get out of this without my powers.

The silence of the walk was unnerving, and the farther we climbed, the more the tension rose. The heat off the lava flows slowly choked us.

The mountain rumbled and the hallway wall ahead exploded inward, and a long sparkling white body followed it through. The firewyrm was far bigger than Scar, easily the size of a small elephant, only longer. It swung its head toward the cowering elementals.

"Fiametta, you go too far this time." He, and it was most definitely a 'he' by his deep voice not to mention his well-endowed male bits that hung low between his back legs.

Fiametta faced him, her hands on her hips.

"Kill it."

Of course, she couldn't understand him.

"Stealing our children, you filthy Salamander," he roared, his voice loud enough that the walls and ceiling shook, rocks tumbling around us. I cringed and jiggled the two kids as they began to cry.

He roared again. This was going to get ugly if no one did anything, which by the way, Fiametta's Enders started forward with their weapons would be the wrong kind of "anything."

"Stop," I yelled, placing the two children on the ground

before running forward. I held my hands up. "Stop it, both of you."

As if that was going to work. The firewyrm lunged forward, snapping at the Enders, his teeth as needle sharp as Scar's had been, only ten times as long. Two Enders disappeared into his mouth with two crunches each. The remaining Enders backed until they were right in front of their queen.

"We cannot take him like this," Maggie said. I hadn't even realized she was with the group until she spoke, her hair pinned under a tight skullcap of black leather.

"Cactus," Fiametta called, "blast him."

That was the moment it became very clear why Cactus was so important to her. He could damage the firewyrms where the Salamanders with their fire only could not. His connection to the earth would allow him to actually puncture their hides.

Cactus was at her side and he shook his head. "This is not a fight I can help you with."

The big firewyrm advanced on Fiametta and she held up her hand. He ignored her.

"You think you rule here, but your fear is what rules this place. You are no queen." The lizard snarled and leapt forward with his mouth gaping.

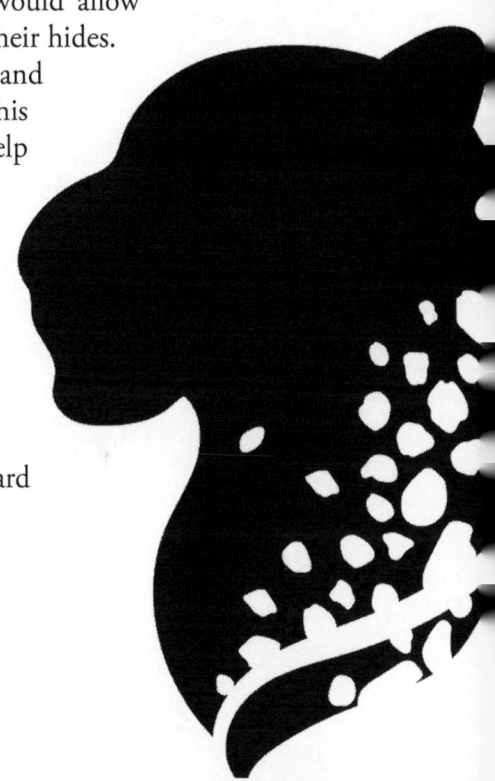

Chapter 22

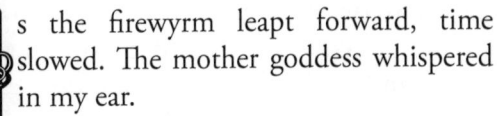

As the firewyrm leapt forward, time slowed. The mother goddess whispered in my ear.

Save her, Lark.

Damn it to the seven hells and back, this was not my fight. And yet, I didn't hesitate at the mother goddess's command. I jumped in front of Fiametta and held up both my hands, as I dropped to my knees.

"In the name of the mother goddess, stop!"

I waited with my head bowed and my whole body tingling with apprehension. Hot breath that smelled faintly of jasmine and chili peppers swirled around me.

"Who do you think you are that you can stop me with words? Are you like the other one?"

Like Fiametta? The firewyrm lowered his face so we were eye to eye.

I didn't lower my hands. "Fiametta is a bitch, a

liar, and a manipulator. She's tried to wipe your people out, punished me with the intention to end my life, and in general being a grade A bitch."

He chuckled. "Yes, all of those things and more. Why do you stop me then from snapping her in half and using her bones to pick my teeth?"

I slowly lowered my hands. "Because the mother goddess wants her alive for some unknown reason. And as her chosen one, I will do all I can to make sure her wishes are fulfilled. If it were my choice, I would let the queen die and another take her position."

He pushed his face forward until we were nose to nose. "You are the one who saved my son and tried to revive my daughter. Spirit walker, your heart is too big for your body."

The firewyrm shook his head at the queen. "Fiametta, only because this one," he tipped his jaw toward me, "intervenes and speaks on behalf of the mother goddess will I spare you and your people. But I want my children back."

I dared to stand. "The Salamanders have missing children too. Someone is killing them."

He shook his massive head, the horns that swept over his neck shimmering from side to side. "Sucked into the lava?"

I nodded. "Yes."

"Then they are not dead. It is how our children were taken too. I feel their hearts beating yet. Come to my nest, and perhaps we can find them, Spirit Walker." He backed up, his body disappearing into the hole he'd created.

Around me it felt as though a collective breath was released and silence reigned for a few seconds longer before several voices at once broke out.

"How did she stop him?"

"What did they say?"

"Why didn't the queen kill the wyrm?"

I turned slowly, meeting Fiametta's gaze. Her emotions were not written on her face like others.

Fiametta lifted a hand. "Larkspur. You are the half breed bastard child that Basileus has kept hidden from the rest of us. Correct? You are Ulani's child." The unspoken question was, are you a Spirit Walker?

No point in denying the truth now. "Yes." I didn't take my eyes from Maggie.

"Then we will discuss this once we are outside the mountain. For now I will trust you, not only with my home, but with my families' lives," the queen said, as she gave Maggie a look that stopped her in her tracks.

Fiametta turned and looked at her people. "We will exit through the main entrance, and once outside I will send some of my Enders to deal with the wyrms and the lava."

No one argued with her, not even the Enders. I slipped back to where I'd deposited the two kids and went to scoop them up. They smiled, reaching for me, but I was pushed away, shoved hard enough from the side that I went to my knees. A big man, his red hair shorn close to his head and enough muscles on his arms to fill out three men's sleeves glared down at me.

"Don't touch them, you filthy wyrm lover."

He picked the kids up, their eyes wide as they stared back at me, and strode away. The Salamanders flowed around me as if I were an island in a stream. They stared at me, the coldness of their eyes like ice against my skin.

Peta found me, her charge gone from her back. "They took her from me too," she said before I could ask.

Ash waited for us, his arms also empty. "Me, too."

"Guilty by association," I murmured, as I pushed myself to my feet. Peta snorted and shook her body, shrinking to her housecat form. I held my arms out and she leapt up to me.

"You can carry me."

Laughing softly, I placed her on my shoulder. "Thanks, I appreciate the vote of confidence."

Falling into step beside me, Ash shook his head. "This seems too easy. Whoever is doing this, blocking them from their element wouldn't just let them out."

"You think it's a trap?"

He nodded. "I'm sure of it."

Walking at the back of the long line of Salamanders, I did a head count. Fewer than five hundred souls, and that was counting the injured being carried. A trap for five hundred people . . . if they couldn't get out of the mountain, and they were blocked from their abilities, what would happen when the lava reached them?

They'd all die.

The line stopped moving and I held back, standing ten feet behind the last Salamander.

Peta sat up straight on my shoulder, looking over everyone's head. "Why aren't they moving?"

I shrugged. "Maybe Ash is right and the door is stuck." The words popped out of me, and the Salamanders closest to us turned back to stare at me. Worm shit, I had to learn to keep my mouth shut. Peta stood up, her front paws on top of my head.

"I think that's exactly what has happened. You need to get up there, you two."

Reluctantly I pushed my way forward through the crowd. Easily enough, they parted around Ash and me as though we were diseased.

The front of the crowd was Maggie, Fiametta, and Cactus who was shaking his head almost violently.

"I can't reach that side of my powers, my queen. I'm sorry," Cactus said. Fiametta's frame shook and at first I thought perhaps she was angry. It was only when I saw her face that I realized she was crying.

The queen of fire, hard as all the granite in the world was crying.

Fiametta saw me, her blue eyes shimmering with tears. "And you two, can you open the mountain?"

Ash stepped forward first, laying his hands on the large black door. I knew what lay outside, an orchard of cherry trees forever in blossom with the heat of the mountain. Ash's arms showed nothing, no lines of power, no traces of green. He shook his head. "I'm sorry."

Now, my turn. I stepped forward reaching for the power of the earth even as it slid away from me. Teeth gritted, I put my hands on the door and bowed my head.

Voices behind me rippled over my ears. What's she doing? Does she really think we would trust her? Their words were the fuel I needed, the anger at their distrust flowed through me and I reached for my connection to the earth. The power flared and I pushed it into the door, spreading it wide with a grinding screech.

I let go of the door and it immediately began to swing closed. Grabbing hold of my power once more I drove it into the door a second time. Sweat broke out on my head as I held it. In front of me were the cherry trees, the scent of their blossoms blowing into the tunnel along with a few loose petals that scattered around my feet.

"Hurry, get them through!" I yelled. Peta clung to me, her nose in my ear.

"What's happening?"

Through gritted teeth, I spoke as the door groaned. "Someone is pushing the doors closed as I'm holding them open." There was only one person it could be: that female in the black cloak, Blackbird's lackey.

Closing my eyes, I held the doors, my entire body shaking with the effort. A hand touched my arm.

"Let it go, Lark," Ash said.

They were through, that was my only thought as I relaxed my hold on the door. It slammed shut with a thunderous boom that shook the walls.

Breathing hard I put my hands on my knees for a moment before straightening and turning around. I stared at the scene in front of me. Not one Salamander less was in the group.

"What the hell is wrong with you? Why didn't you go through?"

"How can we trust you?" Maggie said, putting her face right into mine. "You could have crumbled the archway on top us as we walked through."

There was more than a murmuring of assent more like a roar of agreement.

The mother goddess's words about my father came back to me. Fear would stop people from trusting even those who only wanted to help them.

"You all just signed your own death warrants," I said softly, fatigue hitting me hard. Or maybe it wasn't fatigue, but sorrow, an ache that even when I tried I wasn't able to help them. Because deep down, no matter how much they hurt me or treated me like worm shit, I couldn't stand by and watch them die.

Fiametta motioned for me to follow her a few steps away. For the first time, her eyes showed the strain she was under. "Larkspur, I will beg if I must. I cannot stop the lava flows."

I frowned at her, anger building once more. "You could have made them go through the doorway. You could have been the first one through and shown them the way out and this would now *not even be a discussion*."

Her face was carefully blank. "You are right."

My eyebrows shot up. "Little late for that, don't you think?"

Her lips pursed and then softened, but there was no time for her to answer me. Behind us came the cries of her people and the splashing of lava as it reached the back of the line. People pushed forward, screaming, crying, and begging.

I was jammed against the door along with Fiametta. They would take the doorway now . . . if I could open it.

Fear raced along my synapses as I put my hands on the slick back material once more. There was no room for anger inside the fear that snapped through me, biting at every thought and breath I had.

"Peta, help me," I whispered. "I can't reach the earth unless I'm angry."

"Ash," she called out, "Cactus, get over here."

The two men pushed through, climbing over people to get to me. Screams echoed up the tunnel as the lava kissed at the heels of those at the back.

Ash and Cactus crouched beside me. "What do you need us to do?"

Peta curled tighter around my neck. "Show her you trust her. That is the key to breaking through these final bonds she carries."

Cactus didn't hesitate, but wrapped his arms around me from his side, pressing his lips into my hair. "I trust you to save us, Lark. You can do this."

From my right side, Ash placed his hands over mine. "Larkspur, you truly are the best of us, don't doubt it."

Shaking, I closed my eyes, tried to block the sounds of people being burned alive as I dug into the part of me that held my powers. Spirit and Earth bound together, a bundle of strength I'd never truly tapped into.

Tears streaked my face as I fought to reach them, struggled to get past the blocks put in place by Cassava and an old anger burned through me.

"No," Peta said. "Let the anger go and hold to the trust and love. That is your way now, Lark. That is the only way."

The warmth of Cactus, the belief of Ash and support of Peta swirled through me and I suddenly understood. The strength I had would change things no matter how I used it, but I had a choice. Just like Blackbird.

For good or for ill, how would my power be seen?

The earth's strength roared through me like never before and I flooded the door with it, blasting it apart and sending the one who would hold it against me flying away. On my knees, with my eyes closed, the rushing of the Salamanders as they flew by me no longer caring who I was, the world seemed to speak to me. Two words, but they meant everything to me.

Well done.

Not the mother goddess though, but a male voice, one I didn't recognize. I slowly opened my eyes in time to see Fiametta stride through the opening. She stopped on the other side. "Hurry, the lava is right behind you."

Her words snapped me out of the headspace I'd been in. I glanced behind to see the lava creeping along the tunnel, glowing its fierce red like the eyes of a demon. I put a hand on Peta.

"The children," I said. "We can't leave them to Blackbird. They were his back-up plan, I'm sure of it. And now he has a reason to use them."

Cactus pulled back from me. "The children are alive? Can we get to them?"

I nodded and stood, a feeling of surety falling over me. "We have to."

With a flick of my wrist, I pulled the doorway down,

plunging us back into the semi gloom of the lava-filling tunnel.

Chapter 23

The lava crept toward us and I faced it head on. "Blackbird, I know you hear me. I don't care what your game is, but I want those children. All of them, both wyrm and Salamander."

A low rumbling laugh filled the air and a dark figure approached us, walking along the top of the lava. The ring he wore obviously protected him from the heat as if he were a Salamander in truth. "Little Larkspur, you lied to me. You said you would leave and I would have Fia to myself. But here you are, standing between her and me. Shame on you."

My jaw twitched. "You can have her for all I care, but you can't be killing children. That I won't stand for."

"Well, good thing they're tucked away then. I'd hate for you to be angry with me." He stopped about twenty feet from us, right at the edge of the lava and leaned forward putting a hand to the side of his face. "The little ones, they will make perfect bargaining chips, you see?"

He lifted his other hand. "But you are in my way, I didn't want to do this, but I *will* kill you and your friends." The lava surged forward and I flung my hands up, the earth exploding in front of us. Below my feet the mountain trembled and I gave a soft apology as I drove a hole downward, tunneling as far as I could. The lava flowed into the hole, splashing at the edges.

Blackbird, if that was even really his name, tipped his head to one side. "Worked past your blocks, did you? Clever girl."

He held his hands out and lines of green flowed up from his hands to his shoulders. So he really was connected to the earth as well. Spirit, earth, water and holding a ring that gave him a connection to fire. But I saw what he was going to do and I held my hands out above us, just stopping him.

The ceiling above us groaned and the weight of the mountain pushed down on me from above.

Cactus let out a low whisper. "Shit, he's going to squash us like bugs."

Peta trembled. "He is an abomination."

Sweat dripped down my arms as I held the mountain back. Gravity was on the bastard's side, though, and that tipped things in his favor. A sharp wind snapped through the cavern, throwing all four of us back against the rubble of the door. My concentration broke for a split second and the rocks began to fall in earnest.

I couldn't think of anything to do other than to get farther away from the ceiling. "Hang on!" I yelled as I opened the earth below us, dropping us into a slide as I smoothed the ground around us turning it into a slope that allowed us to fall without freefalling. Above, the rocks tumbled, and a few slid down the slope with us. Pushing my power out ahead like a burrowing mole, I was able to keep us out of the worst of it.

Tumbling to a stop, I looked around, or tried to. We were in complete and utter darkness.

"Cactus?"

"I'm here," he answered.

I tried to stand but ended up whacking my head. "Ash, talk to me."

A low groan from my left turned me around. I scuttled forward, my hands finding Ash quickly. "Are you injured?"

"No, just banged up," he said.

The walls around us rumbled and I froze, my hands tangling with Ash's. Peta let out a meow, as she clung to my shoulder. "Lark, you truly are going to be the death of me aren't you?"

I reached for my power, reveling in the fact I could hold it tightly even though our situation was rather dire.

Rock and dirt sprayed around us, and I could suddenly see. A white-scaled head curled toward me. Amethyst eyes glowed as he blew a low stream of fire from his nostrils to light our space. Cactus was covered in dirt, as was Ash. Peta looked actually, not too bad.

"Scar, how did you find us?"

"Heartbeats, I can find yours easily as it beats louder than any other. Come on, I can get you out of here," he said and turned around, tunneling away from us. I scrambled after him. Cactus and Ash hollered at me to stop, to think about what I was doing.

Peta dropped off my shoulder and scooted ahead of me. "Do you really think you can trust him?"

"If he'd wanted to hurt me, he could have let me fall when I was thrown off that damn ledge." I crawled as fast as I could on hands and knees, and still Scar was leaving me in the dust. The tunnel wasn't completely dark as Scar blew fire ahead.

The light grew brighter as the tunnel widened, large enough I could stand. I waited for Cactus and Ash to catch up before moving forward.

What opened in front of me was nothing short of breathtaking. The cavern was shaped like a giant bowl with tunnels branching off in a myriad of places, but that wasn't all that different from what the Salamanders had set up. It was the deep, pool of water in the middle of the bowl surrounded by plant life and small chirping birds I heard even from my position way above.

"This is amazing," I whispered. Scar poked his head up over the ledge.

"Are you coming? My father wants me to lead you to the tunnel that will take you back into the lizard caves."

I slipped over the edge, Peta leapt to my shoulder with a grunt, and I shimmied down the wall before Cactus or Ash had time to protest. I looked up to see them both staring down at me. They shared a glance between them. Ash shook his head and Cactus shrugged.

Peta's tail flicked me in the face. "Pay attention to the wall you are climbing, not the men."

I focused on where my hands and feet were going, placing them carefully until I felt the wall open up again. Using just my arms I carefully lowered myself the rest of the way and swung into the open hole.

Scar sat on his haunches, waiting for me. Cactus and Ash dropped in a few seconds later. The young firewyrm gave Cactus a sidelong glance. "You can only take your familiar with you. The others have to wait here."

I put my hands on my hips. "Take her with me where? What are you talking about?"

Scar flicked his head over his shoulder, his tongue darting

out and tasting the air. "This tunnel leads to the throne room where the cloaked ones are currently discussing how to wipe out all of us. They have the children deep in the dungeons."

"Then why doesn't your father go get them?" I asked, stepping up beside him.

"Because whenever we get close to the cloaked ones we lose our memory of what we do. That is why we've been attacking the Salamanders. We didn't want to, they were making us." Scar shook his head. "You are the only one who can go in, Spirit Walker. The males must stay here if they are to be safe; they could be forced to hurt you too."

I translated quickly for the two men, relaying what Scar had said.

"No, we aren't leaving her." Cactus shook his head.

Ash nodded to me and said, "Understood."

Cactus stared at him. "You would leave her to do this on her own?"

"She has to. What if the other Spirit Walker takes control of you, makes you fight her? What is she supposed to do then?" Ash shook his head. "I know all too well how hard it is to fight the compulsion, and the only way to break it is to be touching Lark physically. How do we fight when we can't let go of one another?"

Ash's words made total sense. Cactus was still not convinced. "Then how come Peta can go?"

Peta sniffed. "I'm her familiar. I'm protected by Lark's abilities, Prick."

"No more arguing, the longer this takes the more chance we have of them escaping," I said. I didn't look back, just walked away. There was a grunt and the sound of bodies hitting the ground.

"Lark, don't do this, they'll kill you," Cactus called out. I straightened my back and kept walking.

Peta swayed on my shoulder. "How little faith he has."

"No, I don't think it's a matter of faith." I followed the shimmering white scales of Scar's back. "I think it's a matter of love."

Chapter 24

The tunnel Scar took me through opened outside the main doors of the throne room where the firewyrm etched into them seemed to wink at us. I was flat on my belly, barely able to squeeze through. The two large statues were directly in front of us and we were concealed behind the queen's flared skirts. Ironic that she'd been hiding the tunnel all along.

"Good luck, Spirit walker," Scar said as he backed away from me, disappearing back the way we'd come. In the semi darkness, the entrance was invisible, perfectly disguised.

Peta shifted to her snow leopard form and padded ahead of me. Her rounded ears swiveled back and forth as she tipped her head to one side in front of the doors. "There is only one left in the room," she whispered.

Swallowing whatever trepidation I had, I eased the

door open a crack and peered in. The smaller of the two cloaked figures sat on the throne, drumming her fingers on the arm rest.

"I will be queen here and this time no one will stop me," she snapped into the air and the words echoed around. Sliding from the throne she strode forward, her cloak swirling out behind her as she slapped her hands on her thighs. Everything she did looked familiar, like someone I'd . . .

"Cassava," I whispered. That was whom she reminded me of. Her inflections of words, the way she walked, and that thigh slapping. All were idiosyncrasies of my stepmother.

She walked away from me, heading to the far side of the room in the opposite direction of the dungeons. I had a choice. I could follow her and see what she was doing, or I could go after the children.

"Peta, get the kids, lead them through the tunnel. Can you do that?"

"I can. But then you will go after her alone, won't you?" Her green eyes crinkled with concern around the edges. "Won't you?"

I wouldn't lie to her. "Yes, but I've stopped her before, I can do it again. Just hurry. Get those kids out."

Peta slipped through the door ahead of me and slunk toward the dungeon as I hurried after Cassava. The door to Fiametta's personal rooms was ajar. I peered through. Cassava was flinging things everywhere, searching . . .for what? Whatever it was Fiametta had hidden. Whatever her ex-lover Coal had been searching for. He must have been working for Cassava and Blackbird.

"Damn you, Fiametta, where did you hide it?" She grabbed the mattress and flipped it off its supports. Taking a swing with one foot, she kicked at a vase to the left of the bed, shattering it. Glass went everywhere, and I saw what she was looking for. Glass pieces settled into the faintest of depressions in the floor. A very subtle handle.

The only problem was, she saw it the same time that I did. I burst into the room as she opened the secret compartment.

"No!" I screamed startling her.

It wasn't enough though. Her hand dove into the hole and came out with a necklace with a big fat emerald teardrop hanging from it.

"It's mine!" She tipped her head back and howled the words.

The lines of power ran a deep dark green up her arms as she yanked the earth out from under me. Or tried to. I saw her intention and scrambled backward, all the way into the throne room. She stalked out after me, the emerald hanging around her neck.

"You aren't strong enough to stop me now, Larkspur. Not when I hold this." She said, touching the large emerald.

"Doesn't mean I'm just going to roll over you dumb cow." I swung my spear out. "Last I checked, you couldn't fight worth shit."

Her whole body stiffened. "How do you know who I am?"

"I'm no fool, I would know you if my eyes were closed, bitch." I circled her, watching, waiting for her to use the depth of power she carried.

The flicker of green at her fingertips and the slight softening of the ground below was the only warning I had. I leapt at her, spear raised and swinging through the air in a perfect arc as the footing below me dropped away.

She squealed like a stuck pig and scrambled backward, flinging her hands at me, the lines of power going wild over her entire body. It was too much, even for her. The earth exploded through the golden floor, rocks and gemstones flying everywhere. One caught me on the back of my hand, numbing my fingers and making me drop my spear. I landed on top of her and rolled us both across the floor.

Physically I knew she couldn't beat me.

A blast of wind smashed into me, tearing me off her, tearing my fingers away from where I'd gripped her cloak. I was thrown hard and pinned against the far wall. I stared at Blackbird.

His body hummed with power, all five colors swirling. Red, blue, white, green and pink.

"Mother goddess have mercy," I whispered. He carried all five elements, he was the child Requiem had wanted to produce with his breeding program. "How are you even possible?"

The question slipped out of me, unbidden as my mind tried to make sense of the impossibility of what he was. He shrugged.

"I have no say in who made me. I was born though, I can assure you of that." He tossed his ruby ring to Cassava. "Here, use this and kill her. I am off to the Eyrie. I expect you to clean this mess up and take control."

Cassava nodded, shocking me. She was taking orders from him? He bent down and kissed her on the top of her head. "Do not disappoint me."

"I won't."

He walked away, humming to himself as he wove all five elements around his body. Five, even without the use of the ring. As he disappeared, I dropped to the ground.

Cassava crept toward me. "You are finally going to get what you deserve, you stupid half breed. And then I will be queen here."

"Big words coming from someone who is bowing to an abomination," I said, keeping my voice even. This was not the time to panic.

She lifted her hands and fire raced from her fingertips

to light up the wall around me. The heat was instant, sweat popping out along my bare skin.

Maybe this *was* the time to panic.

I pulled the earth upward, dousing the flames, but she ignited them as fast as I put them out. Flinging her left hand, the ceiling collapsed on top of me and instantly lit on fire. I pushed the rock off, but the fire crept closer, igniting my hair in places, singeing my clothes.

"This can only end one way, half breed," she laughed, "and that will be with me dancing on your grave."

I had only one option left, I had to use Spirit to stop her. I called that power forth as the fire super heated around me, gold melting into puddles on the floor. I put everything I had into directing Spirit toward her. It's essence wove through me, melding with the beat of my heart, the thrum of my own blood pumping in my veins as I focused on breaking her hold on the two elements.

"Stop!" I yelled at her.

Her feet stumbled to a stop and she went to her knees.

"You will not harm me or anyone else ever again!" I said, and even to myself my voice reverberated. I kept pushing Spirit into her, fear driving me. Waves of Spirit crashed out of me and into her and for a moment I thought she would fall down. Her body went slack, and she dropped to her knees.

She lifted her hands and the fire went out. "No harm, no harm, no harm."

Spirit danced along my synapses, humming softly, a steady warmth that felt so good. A sigh of relief slipped out of me. It was over without anyone being hurt. If I didn't count the burns and bruises on my body.

I walked over to her as I released my hold on Spirit.

There was a pull within my own soul, like something took a long drink of me. It was there and gone so fast I wasn't sure I hadn't imagined it. I sagged for a split second then stood up straight, forcing my body to obey me no matter how badly it wanted to lay down and rest. I would not look weak in front of Cassava. I strode toward her, my legs like jelly.

"You might as well take the cloak off now. It's not like you're hiding from anyone."

Cassava didn't move; she stood like a statue. Defiant to the end.

"Take the damn cloak off," I snapped and still she ignored me. "Fine, do whatever you like. Father will deal with you soon enough." I didn't dare take my eyes off her for fear she would suddenly grab at one of the powers open to her.

With that in mind, I darted forward and jerked both away from her. She didn't protest, barely even flinched as I took both the emerald and the ruby, tucking them under my vest.

No reaction at all. What was going on? Why wasn't she at least saying something?

The doors to the throne room creaked open and I glanced quickly to see Peta creeping in.

"It's safe. She's taken care of," I said, motioning to Cassava. "Actually, she's playing some kind of game here. Won't talk, won't respond to anything I say."

Peta sniffed the air. "I still can't smell her. Can you take that cloak off?"

I reached out and grabbed the cloak . . . or tried to. It dissolved as my hand passed through it, as if it never were. The cloak vanished and what I was seeing couldn't have stunned me more.

Shock hit me like a lightning bolt and I stumbled backward. "No, no it can't be."

In front of me stood not Cassava but my younger sister, Keeda. Her mouth was slack and her brown eyes empty of any emotion, long tendrils of dark brown hair flowed around her face. She looked like a doll, empty and vacant of any sort of life. The ticks I'd seen her, so like Cassava, they were just a daughter's habits learned at her mother's knee.

Queen . . . she'd been fighting to be queen here.

I struggled to breathe and ended up on my knees in front of her as tears trickled down my cheeks. Peta moved to my side. "You used Spirit on her, didn't you?"

"Yes," I whispered. "What have I done?"

Chapter 25

Peta let out a sigh as she drew closer to me. "My first charge, he learned to use Spirit, but it is tricky. A powerful tool. When you use it without really knowing, it can burn someone else out."

"Burn them out?" I stared at my little sister, the blank gaze in her eyes, the dribble of drool falling from her lips. I'd done that. I'd destroyed her mind. "Can it be reversed?"

"I don't think so." Peta butted her head against me but I pulled away. I didn't deserve any comfort. I stood and walked to Keeda.

"We've got to get her out of here and back home. Maybe Niah can help, she knows more than she lets on." Niah was a storyteller in the Rim, but she also knew a lot about things most Terralings had forgotten. Legends, myths, stories that seemed impossible yet were not.

"Perhaps," Peta said, but I knew she only spoke the word I wanted to hear.

Peta turned and walked away, leading the way. I hooked an arm through Keeda's and tugged on her. She took a step in the direction I urged.

We reached the wide doors, stepped through and the skin on the back of my neck prickled. I spun and looked back into the throne room.

No one was there, no one I could see. And yet I felt eyes on me. I looked up at the doors.

All who enter shall be judged, and those found lacking shall be destroyed.

Was that what had happened, some sort of judgment? I looked away from the words, feeling them burn into my soul. Destroyed, that was how I felt, like a piece of me had been pulled apart and smashed in front of my face. Peta shrunk to her housecat form and slipped into the tunnel behind the statues that would lead us back to the firewyrms. I pushed Keeda ahead of me and she went willingly.

Mother goddess, what had I done? What kind of monster was I?

We emerged into the opening where the firewyrms, Cactus, and Ash waited.

Except they weren't the only ones. The missing children were there too. Tinder saw me, his eyes sparkling with mischief. Waving wildly, he ran to greet us.

"Terraling, the bad luck cat saved us. I couldn't believe it when I saw her, but she saved us."

Peta gave a low grumble, but through our bond her pleasure was a warmth that spread through to me. She leaned out and gave Tinder's face a lick. "You're welcome, little lizard."

Ash strode forward, took one look at Keeda and sucked in a sharp breath. "What happened to her?"

I shook my head, unable to say the words, hiding my shame behind a wall of silence. Cactus looked from me to Keeda and back again and my face burned. He would figure it out if anyone would. But he said nothing about her.

Holding Keeda by the arm, I drew her forward. "I have to get her home."

Cactus nodded but he wouldn't make eye contact with me.

The firewyrms took us to a tunnel that led back to the entranceway. Peta went first then Ash. The seven children, including Tinder, piled in after him, excited and chattering like they hadn't been abducted and kept in a dungeon for hours. Resilient little hearts was the only thought I had for them.

I guided Keeda ahead of me, and Cactus brought up the rear, a faint glow of fire over his left hand. Each Salamander child also held a tiny glow above their hands, lighting the tunnel with ease. At least they could reach their element with Keeda and her cohort gone. I hoped that meant they—and the other Salamanders—were finally safe.

The tunnel was big enough for us to walk without crouching, but only in single file, which made it easy for me to ignore Cactus's attempts to talk to me. Three times he tugged at my arm and cleared his throat. Each time I pushed forward a little faster until Keeda was on top of Ash.

Ash glared back at me after the third pushing incident. "Lark, hurrying at this point isn't going to help anyone."

He was right, but I still didn't want to explain what happened to Cactus so when he reached for me a fourth time, I jerked my arm away from him. "I don't want to talk."

"I just want to hold your hand, Lark. To know you really are here and we're getting out," he said softly.

Shame burned me through and through. I reached back for him and he laced his fingers with mine. A soft warmth cascaded through me and eased some of the heartache that hummed within my body. Still though, my mind would not let me forget what I'd done.

I'd destroyed my sister's soul. She and I were not close, and it was obvious that she was taking after her mother. That didn't negate the fact that she was a hollowed out creature, her body intact and her soul missing. My control—or in this case lack of control—over Spirit had done that.

Another minute passed and we were out of the tunnel and in front of the broken doorway. The children ran around, darting like large fireflies in a game of tag. Ash opened his mouth and I knew him well enough to know what was going to come out. He would tell them to settle down, to be serious, and fall in line.

"Let them play," I said softly. "Let them be children."

His eyes met mine and he gave me a slow nod. Then he held his hand up and the rocks blocking the doorway shifted so we could slip into the open air.

Night had fallen, and the moon was high above our heads giving a soft ethereal tone to the cherry trees and the ever-falling blossoms.

The stillness was broken by the cries of the children as they were reunited with their families, the sobs of mothers and fathers as their little ones, thought gone forever, returned to them.

I put a hand on Peta's back. "Good job, bad luck cat. You did that for them, I think now they will have to give you a new nickname."

Peta snorted softly, but said nothing.

Fiametta strode toward us, her eyes going straight to Keeda.

"Who is this?"

No choice now, I had to come up with a lie she would believe. "This is my sister, she was imprisoned by the one who blocked your element and stole control of the lava from you."

Fiametta leaned in and then sucked in a sharp gasp. "Her soul is gone."

Like a punch to the gut I tried to breathe around sharp dig of pain. I'd done that, I'd stolen my sister's soul. Goddess, how could I ever fix this? "It happened in the battle."

Fiametta was talking, a blur of words. Something about being heroes, or judging all Terralings by a few, or giving us a hero's send off. I didn't really hear much of it, just nodded and smiled while my heart and mind reeled.

I'd stolen a soul.

I was a monster.

"What can we offer you, in thanks for saving us?" Fiametta said, her words finally snapping me out of the fog I'd fallen in.

"Stop killing the firewyrms. Make peace with them. They could have left us all to die, they didn't have to help, and yet they did," I said, mulling over my words and then just going with it. "Like us. We could have left you to fight this battle on your own but we didn't. Because we are family, and no matter how much we fight, we need each other in this world."

The Salamanders around us nodded, and my words were quickly passed through the crowd.

"Family," Fiametta said softly. "That is a word I have not applied to the other elements for many years. Yet perhaps you are right. Call on me, Larkspur, if you have need, and

I will call you cousin in truth. I swear on the soul of my unborn child that I will send aid if you ask for it."

Unborn child. I raised an eyebrow at her. "There is one more thing. Cactus is coming with me."

Fiametta's eyes narrowed.

I gave her a tight smile. "You don't need him now, if you make peace with the firewyrms."

Beside me Cactus tensed, no doubt expecting her to command him to stay. But despite her hard ass nature, he'd been right about her. She wasn't an evil bitch like Cassava, just a very tough woman.

"So be it. But I will miss him."

"I will visit." He grinned at her, and her lips twitched with what might have been a smile.

I held my hand out to her, tapping two fingers across the top of my hand in the way that they showed recognition of someone stronger than themselves. "Thank you, and may the mother goddess be with you and all your children."

There was nothing left to say, and within a few minutes we were all inside the mountain once more. Fresh air replaced the heavy heat of the receding lava flows. The Salamanders were already putting things back into place, and the lava had returned to its bubbling river.

Homes were destroyed and personal items had been burned up in the flooding lava, yet even I could see that the damage was not complete.

Blackbird had to have been directing the flow of the lava all along, chasing the Salamanders. There were areas of the living quarters completely untouched.

I wondered how long it would be before any of them truly trusted their element again and willingly stepped into the lava for a swim.

Fiametta directed her people, encouraging them to help those who'd lost everything. To share what they had. She even put one family into her private quarters while their home was rebuilt. I had to give it to her, she was a better queen than I'd thought. Still a hard ass, but a good leader.

Perhaps I just brought out the best in her. Peta snorted on my shoulder, picking up on my thoughts. "Not likely."

Cactus, free from the hold Fiametta had on him went to the middle of the living area, beckoning me. "Will you help me?"

I went to him. "What do you want me to do?"

"Let's show them just what a Terraling is made of, yes?"

At first I didn't understand, until the first curl of green lines rose up his arms and the shoots of grass erupted under our feet. Nodding, I held my hands out and tapped into the earth. With my eyes closed I imagined a garden loaded with fruit and blossoms, vegetables, and living plants of all varieties. The power flowed out of me with ease and the air around us cooled.

Opening my eyes, I struggled not to gasp at what we'd created. An oasis in the middle of a desert was the only thought I had. Exotic trees that could withstand the heat towered over us, and the ground was soft with soil that would encourage growth.

We'd changed the very makeup of the Pit. At least in this one place.

Fiametta came to us in the oasis. "Cactus, why didn't you do this before?" The awe in her voice was rather gratifying.

He shrugged. "Most of this isn't me. This is Larkspur. I just gave her the idea. Most Terralings could barely get a shoot to grow in this heat . . . she gave you a paradise." He winked at me as I gaped back at him.

I'd done all of it?

Fiametta looked to me. "Then I will give you something in return. The truth." She let out a slow breath. "I know the

Enders were not killed by your hand, Larkspur. I've known all along that Blackbird did it. He told me himself in one of his forays into my bedroom. But I needed you. Finley told me how you saved her people when you didn't have to and I . . . I wanted to believe you could do the same here. And while I perhaps went about it the wrong way, I was right. You did save us."

If I thought my jaw had dropped before it was nothing to what it did then.

"You knew."

Two bright spots of color emerged on her pale cheeks. "I did. I am . . .sorry."

Peta bumped her head against mine. "Take it, Lark. You will never hear those words again from her."

Swallowing the remnants of my anger at the Pit's queen, I held out my hand in the gesture of greeting. Fiametta brushed her palm over mine.

"I have no guarantee that Blackbird won't come back. He stole something of mine. A powerful tool." The queen said.

Damn, she meant the emerald. Sweating, I could feel the stone against my skin. Was that why I'd been able to pull so much power and create the oasis? I had no doubt it was the stone that allowed the user to connect with the earth.

Fiametta continued. " . . . I will work with the firewyrms. Perhaps between our two people, we can find a way to protect ourselves against the power of Spirit. But if we don't . . ." her blue eyes all but nailed me to the spot, "I *will* call on you again. And because we are friends now, you will come."

Damn. Friends? There was nothing for me to do but nod until Peta piped up.

"And she can do the same. Call on you for help if she needs it."

Fiametta surprised me by smiling. "Of course."

Cactus touched my arm. "I think we should go."

The ruby ring. I closed my eyes for a moment and slipped my hand under my vest pulling the ring out. "I took this off Keeda. Blackbird gave it to her."

Fiametta gasped and with a trembling hand took the ring. "Do you know what this is?"

"Yes."

"And you would give it to me?"

Peta purred softly, obviously pleased with my decision. "Who better to care for it than the one who carries the same element?"

Surprising me, she swept me into a hug. "I am so sorry I misjudged you, Larkspur."

Goddess, I didn't want to like her. "I saw it in your eyes when you lashed me."

She pulled back. "I did not want to do it, but I saw no other way out. I have to uphold the law. Always."

There was a soft cough and we turned to see her black panther walking toward us. "Fia," he said, "there is such a thing as the spirit of the law, and the letter of the law. You have yet to learn both have power."

She looked away from him and I put a hand on her. "You should listen to him. The only reason I survived is because I took Peta's advice. Your familiar . . . if he cares for you even half as much as Peta cares for me, you are in good hands."

Peta tucked her head against my neck, hiding her face. "Larkspur, how can you know that?"

Fiametta's face tightened and I thought for a moment she would ignore me. She held a hand out to Jag. "Come, be at my side, pet." He butted his head into her outstretched hand, a deep rumble of contentment slipping out of him.

The queen gave me one last nod. "Cactus is right, it is time for you to go."

We backed away, each giving her a bow before we turned and headed to the Traveling room.

No words were spoken, too much had happened in those last minutes.

The Traveling room was still intact, whatever magic that kept the globe spinning and moving in time with the real world had kept it from collapsing under the heat.

Ash handed me an armband as Brand, Smoke, and their three boys entered the room. Smoke gathered me into her arms.

"Bless you, Larkspur. You saved my boy. I know Peta helped, but she wouldn't have if you hadn't been there." She kissed me on both cheeks and then the lips. "You are always welcome in our home." She put a hand on Peta's head. "Both of you."

Peta fairly glowed with pride. Tinder scooped her up and hugged her against his body and she licked his nose. Stryker and Cano tapped their fingers across my hand before backing away.

Brand hugged me with one arm. "Thank you." Just two words, but they held the weight of what almost happened. If he'd gone into the lava, Smoke would still have lost one of her men.

I gave him a tight nod. "Anytime."

Keeda stood beside me, and Tinder handed me Peta who curled up on my shoulder.

"I can't Travel with more than one person," I said. Peta snorted.

"I'm a part of you, I don't count as a separate being."

That was news to me, but I didn't question her. Brand, Smoke, and their boys waved to us from the doorway as we engaged the armbands and the world of the Pit slid into nothing.

My hand was clamped around Keeda and for a moment,

I thought I would see nothing, that her memories would be gone along with her soul.
 Yet, that wasn't the case in the least.

Chapter 26

The throne room was everything she ever wanted: a golden throne, golden floors and ceiling, gemstones everywhere. This was where she would be queen. A smile lifted her lips as she checked the spell that held her cloaking ability in place.

Simple, it was so simple to take the essence of her element and dilute it so the magic was not a power connected to the earth, but a pure power she could use for spells. Not all that different from a supernatural. The smile slipped as the burns on the fronts of her thighs cracked. She'd gone too close to the Pit and had to steal ointment from the healer's rooms a second time.

Soon though she wouldn't have to sneak anywhere. She'd just make a demand and someone would get her what she wanted.

As she ripped through Fiametta's things, her mind wandered. Why did they have to kill Larkspur anyway?

She was a weak half breed with nothing to offer. Why couldn't Mother see that?

Not that it mattered, she would kill her sister and then be done with that chapter of her life. Mother would be so pleased. Perhaps she would come see her coronation as the new queen of the Pit. She could just imagine her mother smiling, proud of her youngest daughter for doing what none of her other children had managed. Kill the half breed and take a throne in one fell swoop.

The memory busted apart as we stumbled into the Traveling room within the Rim. No one was waiting for us. I shook my head, trying to orient myself and push Keeda's memory away. Perhaps her soul wasn't gone, but just tucked away deep within her. Because how could a memory exist where there was no soul to power it?

Cactus drew in a deep breath beside me. "I can't tell you how good it feels to be home."

Ash clapped him on the shoulder. "I'm glad you're here. Perhaps between the two of us we, can keep Lark out of trouble for more than a day or two."

The two men laughed, but I didn't join them. Now home, there were things I had to take care of. Primarily a missing father and the missing soul of my sister. No matter how bad she was, I couldn't leave her in that state.

"Ash, take Keeda to the healer and call for Niah. See if she can help with what I did to her," I barked the order out as I made for the door. "Cactus, go with him."

Cactus grunted. "Bossy, isn't she?"

"You have no idea," Ash answered.

Peta growled at them both. I ran up the stairs and into the main Enders barracks. The room was silent, but of course it was early enough in the day that even the Enders wouldn't necessarily be up.

The farther I got from the Traveling room, the faster my

feet took me until I was full out sprinting across the small distance between the barracks and the Spiral, my family's home and the seat of my father's rule.

The guard on duty at the main doors stared at me with wide eyes and an upraised sword. At first I didn't recognize her, with her hair cut short enough to leave nothing to be pulled back. Even the sides were shaved.

"Blossom," I said her name and she lowered her sword.

"Lark, you're back."

"Is Belladonna here?"

She nodded. "Yes, go on up. She left orders that when you came home you were to be taken to her right away. But . . . how did you get away? We all thought she was off her rocker thinking you'd escape the Pit."

"Long story, no time for it now," I breathed out as I flung the doors open and headed for the stairs that would take me to the sleeping quarters. While this was my family's home, I hadn't actually lived there for years. Not since my mother, my father's mistress, had been killed by Cassava.

There was another guard on Belladonna's door, and I *did* recognize him right away. Coal.

"I need to speak to my sister.

Surprising the hell out of me, he didn't question me, just stepped aside. "She's crabby when you wake her up suddenly."

He sported a black eye. I couldn't help the laugh. "You tried to make a move on her?"

His eyes narrowed as I pushed through the door, shutting it tightly behind me. "Bella, wake up. I'm home."

She sat bolt upright in bed, her hair a mess and her nightdress tangled around her body. "Lark, thank the mother goddess, you made it out. What took so long?"

I let out a breath. "Long story. But before I do say anything, this is for you." I pulled the emerald necklace out and slipped it over her head. "It will boost your connection to the earth, but you will have to practice. It is a weapon, Bella, and I am trusting it to you. Use it only to protect our family."

Her hand trembled as she took it and slipped it on. "I won't break that trust."

"I know." I let out another slow breath. "The Pit, the traitors there . . . Keeda was in on it."

Bella gasped, a hand going to her mouth. Slowly she dropped it. "Is she alive?"

I sat on the edge of the bed, finally allowing myself to feel the full weight of what happened. "Not really. I . . . burned her out." In halting words, I explained what had happened, and what Spirit had done to our younger sister. Bella reached out and wrapped her arms around me and I let her, lowering my head to her shoulder.

"I should have known better." A sob ripped out of me. The horror of what I'd done wouldn't leave me. I wasn't sure I could ever close my eyes again and not see the vacant stare of my little sister looking back at me.

Bella held me tight. "Would you have died if you'd not used Spirit?"

I mulled the question over rehashing the fight in my mind and seeing once more that there had been no other way. Peta would have been too late to help me and there was no other weapon I'd had that could have stopped Keeda from killing me. "Yes, I would have died. But I could have held back. Should have held back."

"This is not your fault, Lark. You can't be expected to protect yourself and others, and not hurt those who attack you, even if they are your siblings. And you are still learning how to use Spirit. This was an accident." She let me go. We sat in silence for a moment, a silence that I dreaded the breaking of.

"I know you are worried about Keeda, but there is a

larger problem. Father is still missing," she said. "We can't find him anywhere. We're thinking . . . about using a Tracker to find him."

I blinked several times. "We?"

She blushed. "Okay, I was thinking of using a Tracker to find him. Your friend, Griffin, suggested it and I think he is right."

"That's breaking rules, Bella. Rules the mother goddess put in place for a reason. We aren't supposed to even contact those in the supernatural world, never mind seek them out." I stared at my sister, but she was right. We had to find Father, no matter what happened.

I stood. "That's what you're asking me, isn't it? To find a Tracker and use them to find Father? To break the rules."

She sat up straighter, a strange sort of royalty coming over her. "Yes, Ender Larkspur. I am asking you to do whatever you have to do to save our king. Save him, even at the expense of your own soul and the possibility of banishment. Will you do it?"

I looked into her gray eyes, saw the love for our father, and the love for me as her sister.

I went to one knee and bowed my head. "It will be done."

COMING SOON

COMING EARLY 2016

WINDBURN
(THE ELEMENTAL SERIES, BOOK 4)

Authors Note

Thanks for reading "Firestorm". I truly hope you enjoyed the continuation of Lark and her family's story, and the world I've created for them. If you loved this book, one of the best things you can do is leave a review for it. Amazon.com is where I sell the majority of my work, so if I can only ask for one place for reviews that would be it it – but feel free to spread the word on all retailers.

Again, thank you for coming on this ride with me, I hope we'll take many more together. The rest of The Elemental Series along with my other novels, are available in both ebook and paperback format on all major retailers. You will find purchase links on my website at www.shannonmayer.com. Enjoy!

About the Author

Shannon Mayer lives in the southwestern tip of Canada with her husband, dog, cats, horse, and cows. When not writing she spends her time staring at immense amounts of rain, herding old people (similar to herding cats) and attempting to stay out of trouble. Especially that last is difficult for her.

She is the *USA Today* Bestselling author of the The Rylee Adamson Novels, The Elemental Series, The Nevermore Trilogy, A Celtic Legacy series and several contemporary romances. Please visit her website for more information on her novels.

http://www.shannonmayer.com/

Ms. Mayer's books can be found at these retailers:

Amazon	iTunes
Barnes & Noble	Smashwords
Kobo	Google Play

Printed in Great Britain
by Amazon